LOVE NOW—KILL LATER

Rebecca and Ian lay in each other's arms. Their lovemaking had been good, lasting two wonderful, yet exhausting hours.

"You're none the worse for wear," Ian remarked casually, his hand exploring her body in a wonderfully amorous way.

"I could take that as an insult," the White Squaw answered in a dreamy tone. "But I won't. You're the same, too. Only better, always and every time, better."

"My, what a fountain of compliments you are tonight. Is it because you haven't seen me in a long time?" Ian teased.

"Enjoy it while you can. When we locate Roger Styles there won't be time for this."

"Why not?"

"Too busy chasing and trying to corner him, that's why," Rebecca replied.

Ian tensed, his voice changed harshly. "So you can kill him, as well?"

"If necessary. What's the matter, Ian?"

"Even if my spirit isn't strong when it comes to the matter of our love, I still am a minister of the Gospel. Murder is a mortal sin. I can't condone your having it on your soul."

"Ian, it's my soul. Not to worry. Let's not dwell on what hasn't happened as yet. I'm more interested in what's going to happen now," Becky purred.

A brief second later, Rebecca squealed in delight. For the moment Styles could wait—but just for the moment. . . .

#12

WHITE SQUAW

BALL AND CHAIN
—— BY E.J. HUNTER ——

ZEBRA BOOKS
KENSINGTON PUBLISHING CORP.

Special thanks to Mark K. Roberts for his valued assistance.

This book is dedicated to Gary Cartwright, a good friend, whose patience and understanding have made it possible to continue with the saga of Rebecca Caldwell.

Intermarriage among the [Diegueño] tribes and men or women of San Diego and the ranchos was not uncommon. The process of "Christianization" by the Spanish can in part account for this. The treatment afforded to the women was much better than among captives of other tribes. It fell to fiercer, more warlike bands to inflict severe hardship.

—Cecil C. Moyer
Historic Ranchos of San Diego

Chapter 1

Cheeky jays scolded from the dark green foliage of the huge live oaks. Congregations of somber ravens looked on and occasionally cawed their displeasure. Flocks of the tiny blue-black birds called "one bites" by the native population, who featured them in their stew pots, flitted nervously through the foliage. They skittered away when the men climbed into the branches to shake loose a shower of acorns. Below, women and children gathered the abundant acorn fall. Soon the rains would be coming, and after that, the snow. Before then, the pulp would have to be ground and the bitter flavor leeched from the paste. Then the mash would be set out to dry before being made into flour.

There would be lots of *chawee* baked this year. Many of the giant woven reed baskets had already been filled. The slightly sweet, nut-flavored bread would fill the bellies of the people through all the long, cold moons to come. A lighthearted spirit infected the workers as they gathered the bounty.

At some distance from them, a dozen grim-faced men watched the activity. Rudolfo Mateo, leader of the group, curled his thick lips downward in a sneer of contempt. *Estupido Diegueños*, he thought. They do not

7

know how to fight. They never have. They don't even have anyone watching in case of danger.

Fools. Going miles from their reservations to gather acorns. *Chingada!* They are so bitter. Who would want them? Only the stupid Diegueños. There was more than one tribe among these people, Rudolfo knew. The placid, gatherer Indians of the region had been easily incorporated into the Spanish mission system. As was the custom of the friars, the natives received the name of their parent mission for a means of classification and record keeping. Thus, the Kamia, Ipai, and Tipai of the mountains and lowland valleys under the administration of the Mission San Diego de Alcála became known as Diegueños.

When Mexico won its freedom from Spain, an event Rudolfo recalled proudly, nothing changed for the Indians. Then came the *gringos*. *Hijo de la chingada!* So ignorant, they knew nothing of the people here. Even now the border between the two countries, represented by Rudolfo's home of Baja California and the Yankee state of California, leaked like a sieve. That was what made it so easy for him and his men to cross over and reap big rewards in the form of human livestock.

"Compañeros," Rudolfo whispered softly. "It is time for us to move in. Remember, be swift and be cruel."

Rebecca Caldwell stood at the barred front wall of her cell in the territorial jail at Yuma, Arizona. She clinched the flat, iron slats with such force that her knuckles whitened. Frustrated, she knew that U.S. Marshal Oliver Warren, didn't believe a thing she had told him over the past day. Yet, she also realized she had no choice but to try to convince him.

"Please, Marshal Warren. A person is considered innocent until proven guilty, isn't that correct?"

"Yep," the lawman allowed sparingly.

"And I have a right to be confronted by my accusers, isn't that so?"

"Ummmh."

"Well, then, if you can't bring James Morton here, would you mind describing this treasury agent for me? I've a strong suspicion who it really is, and if so, you've been taken in."

"Not likely. I saw his credentials myself," Warren returned in an unprecedented flood of words.

"*Please.* Do it anyway?"

"Well . . . he was close on six feet tall. Had a bit of a paunch. Graying hair and gray eyes. Skin color on his face looked as though he might have shaved off sideburns lately."

"Did he have a scar? Here, on his chin?"

"Humm. As a matter of fact, he did."

Fire glowed behind the sky-blue irises of Rebecca's eyes. "Roger Styles."

"Nope. Papers said he was James Morton."

"All the same, that's Roger. Marshal, let me tell you about Roger Styles. He's wanted in seven states and three territories, for crimes ranging from murder to abduction, bank robbery, and white slaving. He used to direct, although from behind the scenes, a gang of some forty ruffians, led by Bittercreek Jake Tulley. A number of years ago, Jake and his gang, including my uncles Ezekial and Virgil, traded my mother and me off to the Oglala, in exchange for their own lives.

"My mother died in captivity. After five years, I managed to escape. Since then I've been hunting down those responsible. Some have gone to prison; most died. In fact, to the best of my knowledge, only Uncle Ezekial and Roger Styles remain."

"If what you say is true, you must have had a great deal of help."

"No, not so much as you'd expect," Rebecca evaded,

9

careful to protect the identities of Lone Wolf and the others who had aided her through the years.

In particular, she knew, it wouldn't do to make it known that at one time needed assistance had been given to her by Frank and Jesse James. Or that she had been at the Little Big Horn, in the Oglala camp, when Custer met his fate.

"All the same," the marshal protested, "you came in here dressed like an Indian squaw, just like Agent Morton said."

"Not *Agent Morton*—it's Roger Styles. Why shouldn't Roger know that? His gang gave me to the Sioux, and I wear these clothes because they're comfortable. I've been chasing Roger for over two years. Marshal, I don't know what I can say to convince you. There . . ." Rebecca began reluctantly, "there's a gentleman in town who knows me. He can vouch for what I say about where and what I've been doing for the past month."

Warren cocked a sandy brush of eyebrow. "Oh? What's his name?"

"Ian Claymore. The Reverend Ian Claymore, to be exact. I'm sure you know all about the wagon train that came in yesterday. The people had been attacked by Piautes, then had to escape from a pack of religious zealots in the mountains of Nevada Territory. Since shortly after that Indian attack, I have been with the train."

"Aah. There was another white Indian came in with those folks, right? Feller named Baylor, is it?"

"Brett Baylor." Rebecca sighed in resignation. "Brett, though he prefers to be called Lone Wolf, has been helping me from the beginning to bring Roger and his gang to justice."

"Ain't much justice if they ain't tried and hung proper."

"Marshal Warren, have *you* ever lived five years among the Sioux?"

"Uh . . . no."

"If you had, you'd understand. They have a much surer and more immediate means of seeing justice done. What is done is done. Nothing can change that. All I want you to do now is to find Ian Claymore and talk to him. Brett Baylor, also."

Marshall Warren studied on the situation for a while, and on his prisoner. She had a clean wholesomeness about her. Hair glossy, long and black, clear, slightly bronze complexion, a white, even smile, full, inviting lips and high cheekbones. Nice shape, too, he considered, admiring the swell of her firm, round breasts in the white elkskin squaw dress, the dramatic sweep of her torso, and tempting flare of her hips. A lovely package, indeed.

"It's hard to say no to a beautiful woman, Miss Caldwell. I, ah, I'll do what I can."

"Thank you, marshal," Rebecca replied, relief evident in her tone.

He'd have supper first, Oliver Warren considered. Then he'd try to look up this preacher and the white Indian, Baylor. It might prove interesting. *If* they had anything worthwhile to tell him.

"Eeee-yi-yi-yi!"

The shrill vaquero cry sounded from a dozen throats as the bandits crashed their mounts through the brush and into the relatively open, tree-dotted meadow. Many of the Diegueño women and children froze in stooped postures, eyes going wide and round in shock. Separated from their few weapons, the men in the trees could only cry warnings.

"Xiiqu! Xiiqu!" they shouted, then repeated. "White men! White men! *Mesxapu-ly piya' wilitc!"*

Others, accustomed after two hundred years to the language of their conquerors, called out in Spanish. *"Los bandidos mejicanos! Adalante, vaminos!"*

Whatever the tongue, the frightened Indians followed instructions to fly from the badness. They scattered like harried grouse. Small legs churning, the children wailed in fright and sought to evade the tightening circle of bandits. A few shots blasted through the splendid afternoon.

An old man fell, clutching his breast. Blood gushed from between his fingers. At a short distance, a child of three began to flop about like a decapitated chicken when his head exploded outward from impact with a large-caliber slug.

"Let none of them escape!" Rudolfo Mateo bellowed. "Get the men, the young men. Get the *mujeres* and the children over ten years. Kill all the rest."

Here and there, a bronze-skinned warrior resisted. Little puffs of smoke preceded the ignition of their outdated flintlock rifles, and arrows made ghost-whispers through the air. A bandit to Mateo's left howled, more in rage than agony, when a shaft buried in his right thigh. He grunted as he paused and snapped off the offending object, then swung his six-gun toward his assailant.

The heavy Obrigón, a Mexican copy of the model '72 Colt, belched flame and smoke, and a fat .45 bullet smashed into the chest of the Diegueño. Slightly built, the youth flung backward and crashed into a mossy granite boulder. A young man named Atimm imai, or Dancing Bow, sighted his Pennsylvania rifle as he eared back the hammer. A gentle squeeze did the rest.

Flint struck the frizzen, sending a spark into the priming powder. A puff of white smoke rose from the flash in the pan an instant before the flintlock detonated. With a long lance of orange flame, the 50-caliber ball sped toward another bandit.

It struck him in the forehead and blood squirted from his nose and ears. The Mexican outlaw reeled in his saddle a moment, then wilted to one side and fell with a heavy thump. Suddenly twelve more bandits appeared. Like expert cowboys, they circled and closed the gaps. Six-gun and Winchester fire became a steady, crackling snarl. Cries for mercy, in Diegueño and Spanish, rose from the helpless victims.

Old women and men crumpled to the leaf-strewn ground, their life force spilling out in crimson streams. Swiftly the bandidos closed in, gunning down the frightened natives. Above the tumult, the shock-numbed Indians heard the wild, maniacal laughter of Rudolfo Mateo.

"*Yi-ja, yi-ja!* Round them up, *mí compañeros*, like *vacas*. Half of you dismount and disarm them. Keep a close eye, *amigos*. They are tricky, these *indios*."

"*Umau', umau',*" a pretty young mother cried when a rugged-faced Mexican yanked her infant daughter from her arms.

Hefting the squawling baby by her ankles, the bandido swung her through the air in a level arc. When the child's body crashed against an oak tree, the mother shrieked and fell in a swoon. Gunshots crackled here and there as the border raiders dispatched the remaining old people. Three young girls, still pretty, unmarried and virgin, quailed as a vicious quintet of Mexican marauders closed in on them. Grinning beneath a luxurious spill of mustache, which exposed yellowed, rotting teeth, one bandit speculated on their prize. Then he pointed.

"*Esta primero,*" he commanded curtly.

Sakwi-lau trembled at the rough touch of the Mexican's hands. Two of them dragged her away from her

13

companions and began to rip apart her dress.

"*Umau', umau'*, no, no," she pleaded in Diegueño, Spanish, and English. Mockingbird had no doubt as to what fate awaited her.

She twisted and jerked in their cruel restraint until they brutally shoved her to the ground. One of the bandits eased onto his knees, between her outstretched legs and opened his trousers.

With a gasp of shock and revulsion, Sakwi-lau gazed intently at the rigid, reddened shaft of his *meri*. His hand encircled it and he stroked it gently. Slowly, he lowered himself.

She felt the pressure of his *meri* against her secret place and thrashed about to evade the inevitable. He thrust with vigor, and Mockingbird screamed.

"*Au! Au!*" she moaned as she felt the huge, fiery bulk of his member driving into her dry and unwilling flesh. Oh, how it hurt, truly like fire. Would it ever stop?

"Have your fun, *compeñeros*. Only do it fast. We must ride for Baja. What a fine take we made today. We'll be rich from selling these," Rudolfo Mateo boasted. "The *mujeres* into the *putaria* at Mexicali, the boys and young men to the mines. Don Pablo will be proud of us, *verdad*?" he concluded to his number one henchman.

Manuel Guerron produced a lopsided grin. "*Ay, sí. El Coronel* will be most pleased."

"And we shall have many gold pesos to jingle in our pockets."

Chapter 2

In the sedately elegant dining room of the Horton House, located on the plaza in New Town, not far from San Diego Bay, Roger Styles took the chair offered him. In a prolonged moment of silence, he studied the dark, bearded, distinguished-looking man across from him.

"Thank you for inviting me, Mr. Horton."

"I'm Alonzo to my associates, Roger. I've been meaning to get together with you since you first made an investment in my enterprises. A rather substantial commitment, I might add."

Horton took in the man opposite. Roger Styles had more the look of a used-buggy salesman than a financier. Although heavily pomaded, his hair had a lackluster quality, far too much gray for his apparent age. The lines of Roger's face evidenced some considerable familiarity with dissipation. Word of the man's manner of approach in conducting business had reached Alonzo, also, and he didn't particularly care for what he'd heard.

"Ah, thank you, Alonzo. I'm beginning to learn quite a bit about your county. Sort of getting my feet wet, so's to speak."

"Not in the bay, I hope." Alonzo tried for lightness.

"Ah-huh. No, no. Figuratively, only. I never realized

how vast an area San Diego County covered. Why, it's a good two-thirds of all Southern California. Everything from Los Angeles south. Imagine. Quite an expanse for development. How quickly do you feel, ah, our enterprise can expand to take fullest advantage?"

Soft, pink hands, with fingers that writhed like fat worms, lay on the table before Roger Styles. Those, and a certain childlike pout to his thick, sensuous lips, gave him a boyish appearance, Alonzo considered with distaste. All together he gave him a strong sense of unease. Although he didn't like the public nature of this meeting, Alonzo considered that it might be the best opportunity to put forth his present plan. Reluctantly, Alonzo had to agree that he concurred with his usual associates. Earlier that day they'd had a meeting.

"Damnit, I just don't like the man, Alonzo, simple as that," Hiram Wayland had declared forcefully. "Granted he has a shrewd business acumen. But, there's something about Roger Styles that makes me uneasy. He can draw a crafty plan well enough. Unfortunately, when it comes to executing it, he has all the tact of an enraged bull and the finesse of a pregnant buffalo. When his offer to acquire that land in the Pala valley was turned down, he actually said we ought to send around some 'hired guns' to convince Don Alejandro to sell. Can you believe it? He actually used the term, 'hired guns.' He's like a character out of a dime novel."

"There's more," Bertrand Scripps injected. "He dresses too flashily, spends money too freely, and consorts with rather questionable layers of our society. When not actually on the job, the man's crass and vulgar."

"There's even rumors that he fancies rather, ah, young female companionship," Hiram Wayland added. "The bankers, brokers, and developers of our commu-

16

nity should be sober, married, reserved members of society. Roger Styles doesn't fit that portrait."

"What do you propose we do, then?" Alonzo had asked. "Oust him from our organization? Return his money, which we desperately need at this time, with our thanks and a fond farewell?"

"No, no," Hiram hastened to protest. "Yet, there must be something . . . ah, harmless, we can direct him into. Don't you think?"

They all considered the matter for quite a long time, then came up with the proposal Alonzo was about to make.

"Are you ready to order, sir?" a white-jacketed waiter inquired obsequiously.

"Not at the moment, Willard. We will have a bit of sherry. Would that stimulate your taste, Roger?" Alonzo asked.

"Ummm," Roger returned, lost in his own reverie. "Ah, say perhaps some brandy, if you have it? Water on the side."

"Right away, gentlemen."

Willard departed soundlessly across the thick carpet. In his absence, Alonzo leaned forward and began to outline his plan.

"We, my associates and I, have decided that it is time to give you a wider scope in which to exercise your considerable acumen. A development project that will be entirely your own."

"Within your group, of course," Roger replied, his close-set eyes taking on a resentful glitter.

"No. Actually it's an entirely independent operation. There is a Russian, Count Vladimir Korchenko, who has been speculating in land in the South Bay area. His holdings are below Kimball's Rancho de la Nación and north of Rancho Otay. He intended to set up evaporation beds for producing salt. At least, that was one

17

project. He also has bought heavily into uncleared land between the bay and the Mexican border. He believes it will one day become rich farming country. Unfortunately, he has become overextended. Also, relations between his country and ours are not at the best at this time. He is being recalled. As it happens, Wayland, Scripps, and I agree with his ideas. The problem comes in our not being able to expand into that area at this time. There is a way, however, that we all might profit from it."

"And that's where I come in?"

"Precisely, Roger. Naturally, it would entail an additional investment on your part. Not an astonishing sum, a mere thirty-five or fifty thousand ought to do it. In order to enhance your prospects of success, we would be willing to stand behind you with a letter of credit in the amount you have so far invested in New Town Enterprises."

Shrewdness painted Roger's face and slitted his eyes. "At what percentage on my profit?"

"Surely nothing you would find to be a bone of contention."

"Meaning?"

"Ah . . . twenty-five percent."

"Of the gross? Not possible. Not even fifteen."

"Say, twenty-five of the net?"

Roger rubbed his chin, unconsciously massaging the thin scar where Rebecca Caldwell had cut him with her skinning knife. He had other scars, welts on his chest and back from her fingernails, a couple of bullet wounds. For a second, anger flashed behind the heavy lids of Roger's eyes. Then he fought down his recollections and forced a hearty smile.

"You drive a hard bargain, Alonzo. But one that could be met, were you willing to compromise between my fifteen and your twenty-five . . . say, twenty percent?"

Horton's eyelids drooped in a manner that indicated careful rumination. After a moment, he nodded. Roger beamed a smile.

"When would I be able to talk with this, ah, Count Korchenko?

"Tomorrow evening, at seven. At my home. A small reception followed by dinner is on the schedule. You could meet informally that way and establish your own protocol as to business dealings."

Roger became effusive. "An excellent idea, Alonzo. It . . . fits my plans most conveniently. Now, tell me. Would expansion into the South Bay area interfere with my present ambition to obtain and develop land in the eastern part of the county, say from the mountains to the Colorado River, and northward to the San Bernardino Mountains?"

A fleeting scowl crossed Alonzo Horton's brow. "Not so long as you didn't find yourself undercapitalized, like poor Vladimir. One step at a time, I would caution."

"You certainly didn't proceed at such a slow pace," Roger accused.

"Yes. But at the time I began in San Diego, there was no one else doing anything. Land values have risen dramatically. Why, some areas are selling for two dollars an acre. Even options cost a tremendous ammount."

Roger nodded and turned his attention to the gold-embossed menu. "I'll be glad, then, to meet your Count Vladimir. Tomorrow evening will be fine."

So far, Alonzo Horton thought with gratitude, so good.

After the dinner meeting, Roger Styles sat at the desk in the small office he had acquired for himself.

Separate from the Horton Development Corporation, it provided a place where he could arrange the less reputable aspects of his strategy. He turned the brass-bound lamp higher and pored over the papers he had been accumulating.

The salient facts quickly aligned themselves on a notepad, listed in Roger's bold scrawl. Two factions controlled most of the beautiful and desirable land outside the city. First, nearly all of the land under cultivation belonged to the Mexican land-grant ranchos. Obtaining them legally would be entirely too costly. Not that Roger had any qualms about using other means. With that thought in mind, he made a note beside that item. He would look around town for the type of men who made a trade out of unsavory work.

The second faction consisted of the Indians of San Diego County. Land had been set aside for their use since the time of the Spaniards. The tribes held no title, Roger had discovered. All the better. All he needed there was to remove the savages and take over the ground. Recruit more men, he noted on the pad. Potentially, he could acquire nearly two-thirds of Southern California. Roger's eyes glittered with the lust for wealth and power. He'd have to be careful, though, he cautioned his swelling ambition.

Alonzo Horton's New Town Development Company represented a third factor. Horton, Scripps, and a few others represented *the* power base in the county. To buck them too soon would be risky. He'd take the back country first, then move in on the cities.

There were few enough of those. Desert, mountains, a bleak seacoast did not meet the needs of industrialization, at least as it had developed in the East. The cost of transporting machinery made centralization prohibitive. The fine bays from Los Angeles to San

20

Francisco had attracted population. So far San Diego had little to recommend it to investors. With a railroad, that would be different.

Horton wanted a railroad. For the time being, until he could put his real plans into action, Roger did not. Taking over an enterprise of his own, like that of Count Korchenko, would allow him openly to oppose the railroad plans Alonzo Horton and Frank Kimball had recently proposed. Yes, Roger considered, fortune had smiled on him when Horton suggested this move.

A soft knock invaded his reverie.

"Come in," Roger invited, his right hand in the desk drawer, fingers curled around the grip of a Merwin and Hulbert revolver.

Tall and fencepost lean, Dooley Walsh seemed to ooze around the open door. A curly lock of lank, dirty-blond hair hung low on his forehead. He smiled a gap-toothed grimace and fingered the bowler hat he held before him. Three long strides brought him to Roger's desk.

"I found out what you were looking for, Mr. Styles," a soft, purring voice declared, belying the cold killer's look in Walsh's blue-gray eyes.

"Go on," Roger said coldly.

"Seems this Rancho Jamul is a bit under the weather. Strapped for cash money. If any of them could be snapped up cheap, that'ud be the one."

Roger suddenly beamed. He felt a warmth of fellow-feeling toward his primary — and only — henchman. He resolved to get to know Walsh better. With an expansive wave to the only unoccupied chair in the room, Roger rose and crossed to a low cabinet.

"Sit down, Dooley. Let's have a drink. A toast to the future. I'm certainly glad to learn this choice tidbit."

"Why, thank you, Mr. Styles." The left-handed hardcase came as close as he ever did to showing genuine emotion at Roger's remark.

"Call me Roger. There's something new coming up, and we'll be working quite closely together from now on."

"Ochen preyahtnah," Count Korchenko remarked in a deep, rumbling voice. "Pleased to meet you," he repeated in atrociously accented English.

"Thank you, ah, your, ah, excellency," Roger Styles replied.

"Alonzo Ivanovich has told me you are interested in agricultural property. This is so?"

Use of the Russian custom of naming a person by their first name and that of their father threw Roger for a moment, until he realized the count referred to Alonzo Horton. "Indeed I am," Roger responded eagerly.

"Come then, let us partake of a drink and some of the lavish *zahkooske* that Mrs. Horton had prepared for us. Dinner will, I somewhat fear, be a bit late."

Located on a high plateau, above the lower plain on which the commercial district of New Town was being constructed, Alonzo Horton had erected a remarkable Victorian mansion. Its many windows overlooked the bay and the deltalike spread of warehouses, business fronts and hostelries going up in profusion in San Diego. Other fine new homes clustered nearby and soft lights glowed in many a dwelling. Roger, escorted by Count Korchenko, made his way to a white linen-covered side table where a uniformed servant dispensed spirits.

"Votka," the nobleman demanded crisply.

He received a clear liquid in a tall-stemmed glass. Unfamiliar with the beverage, or its effects, Roger requested a brandy. He and the Russian wandered away from the elegantly attired ladies who chatted together in the center of the room. A circular, turretlike bay offered them the semblance of privacy. They saluted with their glasses and sipped. Then Korchenko sighed heavily.

"A regrettable situation I find myself in. The czar squabbles with your president and now my government recalls me to Mother Russia. *Bozhemoi!* Such foolishness. I am a businessman, a speculator and land developer, not a diplomat. It appears that your government does not want a Russian presence in California. Not even for business. So, like two boys in a schoolyard, the representatives of our nations quarrel and exchange insults. They make of something so simple as doing good business *nyeveepolne'emzeya zadachea* — how you say? — an impossible task. I have acquired a great deal of excellent land that will some day become large, profitable farms. So, do they let me keep it for the future? No. I must liquidate my holdings and return to my country. *Upryamye osele'y!*"

"Alonzo said you had invested in land in the, ah, South Bay area and eastward to the foothills?"

"That's correct. Much as I regret it, I'm prepared to sell the entire parcel for, ah, six million rubles."

Inwardly, Roger winced, though he didn't show any change of expression.

"That's, ah, eighty-five thousand of your dollars."

That seemed much more reasonable. Roger affected to look grave, though the actual figure was well within his ability to pay.

"That comes as an attractive offer. I'll have to consider it, of course. Tell me, what do you know of Rancho Jamul?"

Korchenko cocked his head to one side, frowned slightly. "Only that the owner is having money problems. The land is to the other side of the foothills from mine. Lots of Indians out there, also Mexican squatters who have crossed the border. Nothing but rocks and boulders and scrub oak trees. Too poor to farm on a large scale."

Elated, Roger nodded sagely and turned the topic back to the South Bay. "Why is it you're so sure this land you have will become agricultural?"

"Several reasons. The soil's rich, the land flat and mostly cleared of brush now. A cheap labor force is available. Myself, I would have brought peasants, Kulaks and Ukrainians, to work the ground. Another person could use Mexicans. The natives, the, ah, Indians, *da*? The Indians make poor laborers. They don't understand the reasons. They're too individual. Efficient farming takes a collective effort. Someday the whole world will come to realize this."

"The farms in this country are starting to do rather well. They're privately owned and operated," Roger felt constrained to reply.

"What about the blackamoors working in droves on plantations?"

"We fought a war over that recently, Count Korchenko. I'm sure you recall? Slavery is ended in this country and there's never been a peasant class to till the soil for aristocratic landowners."

"My friend, the world's changing around us and we hardly know it. There was a book, written some twenty years ago by a German living abroad in England. His name was Marx. In this book, he proposed that the workers and peasant class should set up a radical new form of government. One in which there were no distinctions of class or status. A *collective* state, in which all shared alike. Utopian, perhaps. Yet, it had such an effect that the czar banned its presence in all the Russias. Even so, I managed to obtain a copy. I'm not so certain that anyone can prevent our hearing a great deal more about this philosophy in times to come. Such theories often become flawed and unworkable when practically applied. But they are pragmatic. The ideas appeal to the indolent and the ignorant masses. Enough of this talk, though. Let's refill our glasses and speak further about my problem in the South Bay Land Trust."

While crossing the room, Roger came to a decision. "I've been considering your proposal, excellency. Provided we can come to some terms regarding the payment of the sum you named, I see no reason we can't do business."

"Excellent! I'd hoped you might see it that way. Here, my good man, refill our glasses. A toast, Roger, to our mutually beneficial relationship."

Roger, beaming, raised his glass. "To your good fortune, Vladimir, and your health."

"Zavahsheh zdahrohv'yeh!"

Yes, Roger gloated, *it was going quite well indeed*.

Chapter 3

Rebecca Caldwell remained behind bars in Yuma. Oliver Warren, the U.S. marshal for the southwestern portion of Arizona Territory, sat behind his desk, listening to the two men opposite him. Their story sounded bizarre enough to encourage disbelief. If half of it happened to be true, then maybe the young woman should be held for an assortment of other charges. The earnest, blond-haired man, Baylor, seemed to be reaching his conclusion.

"One thing for certain, marshal, Rebecca has never had the time, nor the opportunity to learn engraving. She was taken into that Oglala village at the age of fourteen. For five years she remained there. I aided her in her escape at that point. Since then, we've been pursuing the men who put her there."

"From what you tell me, she's responsible for the deaths of some thirty persons?" Warren ran a blunt-fingered hand through his graying hair. "How many of them had been granted due process of the law?"

Lone Wolf shook his head sadly. Always the same questions. "She personally had her hands on the levers to drop three men through the traps at Fort Smith. Judge Parker's hangman allowed her that."

"And?" Curious now, Marshal Warren pressed for more intimate details.

"She found it unsatisfactory."

Warren paled. "My God, how much more personal can you make a kill?"

"Oh, it wasn't that, marshal. It was, she said, distasteful. As though the men who were hanged had no chance at all. She found it cold, detached."

Ian Claymore had never heard of this experience before. It profoundly affected the tall, handsome Scotsman. He knew of Rebecca's calm nature, even under fire, yet he had not realized that she had been entirely serious in recounting her efforts to punish the men who had driven her mother mad and left her at the mercy of a camp of Sioux. He felt compelled to present her in a more favorable light.

"That's not all the story, marshal," the minister offered in mild, deep tone. "Rebecca is a kind, compassionate, understanding person. There was a boy on our wagon train, Toby Andrews. His mother and sister had been killed by the Paiutes and his father wounded. Rebecca sort of . . . mothered him. Consoled the lad and built up his confidence. And Toby's friend from the religious community, Damon Trent, was in great need of affection, security, all the things those animals had driven from their lives. Rebecca provided that. Oh, granted, she's capable of unbelievable feats of violence. Yet, I've seen her weep over the necessity of her acts. And, believe me, it was a matter of being most necessary."

"Hummm," Warren responded noncommitally. "You two paint a strange portrait of Rebecca Caldwell. I have to allow, however, that you do effectively refute the charge of counterfeiting. I wired this James Morton in San Diego and never received an answer. A telegraph message to Denver brought a response that no known warrant was out on such a person. That came in only this morning." His sudden apologetic smile eased the tension of the moment. "So, I suppose there's nothing to do but release her."

Ponderously, the marshal rose from his swivel chair and plucked a ring of keys from the hook on the end of the gun rack. Lone Wolf and Ian Claymore exchanged glances, at once relieved and somewhat smug.

"We're all set up, Roger, like you asked," Dooley Walsh informed his employer.

Roger Styles's cold smile added a special cruelty to his face. "How many of these brush shelters do you say there are?"

"Two dozen, maybe twenty-five."

Under the shelter of a huge oak tree, Roger and five of his newly recruited henchmen waited in the large valley formed by the foothills of the Laguna Mountains. Mount Cuyamaca showed tall and bold above the other promontories. At a distance of half a mile, a Diegueño village had been surrounded by the remaining fifteen waterfront ruffians. More familiar with the deck of a boat than a horse's back, the journey into the big valley had been a painful experience for most.

The killing would soon take their minds off that, Roger considered. He pursed his lips and spoke precisely, a habit that irritated Dooley.

"Well then, make sure the men fire them all. No one is to be allowed to survive."

"Not even the brats? We could sell them."

"And possibly be identified later as responsible for . . . ah, this? No, thank you. I have no desire to see that occur."

"You gonna come up with the rest of us, Roger?"

"At the proper time, Dooley. These, ah, gentlemen and I will insure that no one manages to slip away

28

following your initial attack. Now, let's get about it, shall we?"

Twenty minutes later, gunshots and screams sounded faintly from the direction of the village. Columns of black smoke began to rise in the bright, clear air. Anticipation of the carnage quickened the pace of Roger's heart. He nodded his head in the manner of a signal, and the remaining force closed in from a distance of two hundred yards. Roger released the thong that secured his whip and held it ready. To his right the tall grass rippled in a telltale betrayal of someone fleeing the battle. Roger urged his mount that direction.

A slim boy of some ten years crouched in the waving stalks of grass. His dark brown eyes, wide in a round, flat face, gazed with fright on the broad breast of the horse that drew near to him. He didn't see the motion, and didn't hear the swish and crack until afterward, when Roger unlimbered his bullwhip. The lead-tipped cracker end ripped through Nema's deer hide shirt and he felt a sharp sting where it sliced flesh. He recoiled and raised his arms instinctively in an attempt to protect himself.

Roger swung the deadly weapon again. The small lad cried out in anguish. Roger felt a rush of heat bloom in his loins at the pain he inflicted. The lash cut again.

Nemas tried to whirl away from the deadly braid of destruction, only to fail. The lead tip cut open the back of the boy's garment and left a long, red stripe on his tender back. Another crack and bite of pain. And another. Panting in an ecstasy of torment, Roger closed in, methodically stripping the shirt from the youngster's body.

Eyes aglow with passion, Roger licked his lips, then

29

casually drew his Merwin and Hulbert .44 and shot the terrified child between the eyes.

"Let's go find some more," he commanded.

Sickened by the savagery and excessive bloodshed, two of the riders could not meet Roger's eyes. The six men spread out, circling the Diegueno camp. Sporadic shots popped in the village.

"There's another one," Dooley Walsh called out, pointing out a girl of eight or nine to a bulldog-faced brawler.

He'd recruited the burly longshoreman from O'Banion's on the strip of notorious saloons along the bay. Severely limited in intelligence, the ruffian made up for lack of wit and speed with brute force. Now he turned with an idiot's slack-faced grin to where Walsh indicated.

The girl cringed behind a large basket of acorns. In two strides Hooper made it to her side. He raised the wickedly gleaming longshoreman's hook in his right ham-sized fist and lashed downward with it. So powerful was his blow that the girl was instantly killed.

"Leave the body," Dooley commanded. "There's plenty more to finish off."

Two Diegueño men had found a passable defensive position in a cluster of granite boulders. Others struggled to join them. From there they sent arrows speeding toward their enemies. Not enough, though, for the number of them seemed not to diminish. To all sides, women and children screamed in fright and ran about in confusion. The bodies of their friends littered the ground. Noisily, a bullet screeched off a huge rock and smacked into the side of one courageous Diegueño's head. In the distance, well out of bowshot, the defenders saw three men sitting relaxed on their mounts, taking careful aim with the long-shooting guns. Smoke and flame lanced from the muzzles.

Two more Diegueño men died.

In twenty minutes it ended. The last cringing woman had been found, dragged into the open and shot to death. The final whimpering child had been stomped by a prancing horse. Quailing old men and women went unprotestingly to the darkness beyond.

"Excellent, for your first attempt," Roger Styles praised his men. "We must hurry, though. There are two more villages we can raid before sundown."

Rebecca Caldwell lay back on the crisp, off-white sheets of the big bed in the best hotel in Yuma, Arizona Territory. The dark rings of her puffy aerolas resembled two fanciful moons of some distant, mythical planet. Her nipples, relaxed now after an hour of arduous lovemaking, still protruded impudently from the centers. A pale sheen of moisture covered her light bronze, nude body. Ian Claymore lay beside her.

Languidly, Rebecca examined her lover. He seemed to be all angles and lumps. More so than any man who had ever shared her bed, except for Four Horns, her first and most fondly remembered lover. She had barely turned sixteen when the lusty Oglala youth, only two years her senior, had cast aside tradition, taboo, and her own hesitancy to claim the prize of her maidenhead. And, oh, how wonderful that occasion had been for her. Ian reminded her of Four Horns in many other ways as well.

He had deep, abiding gentleness and love for people. He possessed a quiet strength and assurance in himself. When she suggested some of the more unconventional forms of lovemaking, it embarrassed the sandy-haired Scotsman, yet he participated eagerly. Her hand strayed to the firmly ridged muscles of Ian's lower belly.

"I began to despair that I would never get out of there."

"When I learned where you were, I wanted to go at once. Lone Wolf convinced me to wait until this morning and we'd go together. A show of force, so's to speak."

"I'm glad you did. Ummm. What have we here? Oh, my, it grows when you caress it. How lovely. I wonder how it can be made useful?"

"Becky!" Ian exclaimed, scandalized.

"I know," she responded gleefully, like a small girl with a new toy.

Rebecca rolled so that she straddled the handsome man in her bed. A shudder of joyful anticipation coursed through them both. Slowly she edged backward until she felt the solid contact of his once more rigid phallus. Industriously she encircled it with warm, moist fingers and began to stroke the sensitive tip. Delightedly, she wriggled in impatience. A distant, happy expression filled her high-cheekboned face as she guided the first tender inch into her steaming passage.

Ever so slowly, she joined them. Then, pelvis heaving, she began to drive them both toward an even greater ecstasy than the last time. Bright lights, in myriad blazing colors, cascaded behind her glazed eyes. Harder she worked, thrilling to the perfection of their mutual achievement. Ian began to respond, driving to match her thrust for thrust. The world turned giddy. Rebecca threw back her head, her long tresses slithering against the inner surfaces of Ian's upraised thighs. Her mouth twisted into odd shapes, reflecting the constant assault on her senses that her ardor brought.

"Ayiiiieee! Aaaaah! Now, now, NOW!" Rebecca cried out as the dam broke and they both flooded out in ecstatic completion.

"Don't stop," Ian urged. "Keep going."

"Oh, yes, yes, yes!" Rebecca keened as she surrendered to oblivion.

"You've got over sixty-five fellers workin' for you now, Roger," Dooley Walsh informed his leader the day following the massacre of three Diegueño villages. "That costs a lot to maintain. I've got an idea on how to offset some of yer expenses."

"Wonderful news. What's that, Dooley?" Roger replied in a soft purr.

"Down Sonora way, the Mezkins are payin' five pesos, gold, for Apache and Yaqui scalps. Injun hair's Injun hair to me. Same fer them. Once it's off the head, who's to tell?"

Roger gave Dooley a wolfish grin. "That's inspired, Dooley. I appreciate your concern and loyalty. Only, this time, I'm way ahead of you. Why do you think that small group of five remains behind on each raid? They take the scalps, give them a rough curing and box them up. Then the, ah, product is shipped by stage to an associate of mine in Nogales, Arizona Territory. He sells them across the border to the Mexicans. So, the more we kill, the more self-sufficient this project becomes and the more land will be up for claiming."

Dooley smacked thick lips in appreciation. "You think of everything, don't you, Roger? That's mighty slick. I have to admit I hadn't thought of how to dispose of the hair, once we got it. Who's this associate?"

"Name's Ezekial Caldwell. I've been connected with him in business for some time. Completely trustworthy."

"Yer sure of that?" Dooley gave his boss a slantwise glance.

"Oh, absolutely. Ezekial has use of only one arm. He knows I'd kill him if he ever attempted to hold out on me."

"Nice to have partners you can trust," Dooley said dryly.

"Yes, isn't it. How far north of Pala Valley are we?"

"Some ten miles, give or take a couple."

"Good. If we pick up the pace, we can hit this first Cahuilla village at sunset, take the other three first thing in the morning."

Chapter 4

By long habit, Umeck of the Cahuilla rose early each morning. This day he did not get to see the usual spectacular display of pastel colors as the Sky Father rose out of the desert below and tinged purple the sawtooth ridges of his beloved mountains. The sky hid behind a thick layer of roiling gray, like the troubled thoughts of his mind, Umeck considered. Runners had come, late during the night, with disturbing news.

They declared that a village of his people had been attacked by *haiqo*. How could that be? There had been no fighting in more seasons than anyone could remember. Oh, here and there, a few greedy men might try to run the Cahuilla off a choice parcel of land in order to take it for themselves. Or angry men, what the *haiqo* called a posse, might rough up a few people while seeking someone accused of a white-man crime. But for a village to be attacked and destroyed? Umeck had trouble seeing pictures of such a thing. He stretched his weak old limbs and breathed deeply of the sage-scented air. All the same, no sun, or with its welcome heat, he would have walked to the rim and gaze down onto the desert. Umeck strode out of the cluster of bark and reed-thatch huts that formed his village.

He walked directly into the sinuous coils of Roger Styles's whip.

From behind the ancient man, Roger looped the thin end of the braided leather around Umeck's neck and yanked tightly. The old tribal leader struggled briefly, thrashed his arms and legs, and died.

"That's taken care of," Roger panted. His years of pampered living had taken a toll. "Everyone should be in position. We'll attack at once."

"What was he out here for?" Bert Conlin inquired in a whisper.

"To welcome the morning," Roger answered. "All of the plains and desert tribes have some form of that ceremony. These people must have once lived down on the flats below."

"That's right," Dooley added. "There's Cahuilla who still live down by the hot springs at Rancho San Jose del Valle. They work as cowboys for Don Juan Jose Warner."

"A Mexican named Warner?"

"Naw, Roger. He's from back East somewhere, Connecticut, I think. He just took a Mex name way back when he came here and got a big land grant. That was before the U.S. took California from the Mezkins."

"We've wasted enough time. Go in quiet, get the lodges to burning. Anyone who comes out, shoot 'em down."

Shrieks of agony and terror soon filled the rocky pocket that held the Cahuilla village. Few managed to escape their burning dwellings. Those who did died in a hail of gunshots. Victor Ocatillo, a visitor from the desert band at Warner's Springs, acted with a cool detachment that saved his life.

Lean, hard, and stocky, his dark face lined and seamed by long exposure to the sun, Victor saw no reason to wait helplessly for death to come. He ignored the threat of the flames while he cut his way through the rear of the bark hut in which he had slept. Grasping his weapons, in particular his prized model '68 Winchester repeater, he eased through the opening. Rough edges clung to him and scratched his skin. He dismissed them as unimportant. While women and children wailed and died around him, he swiftly crawled on his belly into the rocks and lay low for a few tense, anxious minutes.

Satisfied he had not been seen, Victor worked his way backward, upslope toward the promise of safety. He would travel south, Victor decided, to the Diegueños. They, too, had suffered much lately. All the while, he vowed that these *haiqo* would be made to pay for the murders.

"Someone is attacking the Indians around San Diego," Ian Claymore announced over breakfast two mornings later.

He laid aside the latest copy of the territorial newspaper and studied the frown lines on Rebecca Caldwell's usually smooth forehead. Maybe he shouldn't have brought it up at this time. Rebecca already felt certain that James Morton, the spurious treasury agent, and Roger Styles were one and the same. Mention of this sort of trouble could fix that conviction in her mind.

"Any information on who might be doing it?" Lone Wolf inquired.

"Who else?" Rebecca fired back. "Roger Styles has to be behind it somewhere."

"You're jumping to conclusions, Becky," Ian chided gently.

"No, I'm not. Roger went from Yuma to San Diego, now there's trouble for the Indians. Who else could it be?"

"But . . . you have no proof," Ian protested, now certain the direction this discussion would take.

"I have all I need for now. Ian, Lone Wolf and I have to be on our way to San Diego by the fastest means. Oh, granted, Roger would cover himself with some sort of legitimate front, one few could penetrate. We know him, though, and once we're given a trail to follow, we can uncover all his schemes."

"The stage is fastest," Ian offered reluctantly. "Only what will you do with your horses?"

"Take them along."

"Becky . . . I . . . is there no way to persuade you not to go?"

"None. I must, don't you see? There's too much coincidence that someone would try to intercept me like this, someone whose description matches Roger's, and not be him. After all, my experience with the man, knowing that he went on to San Diego can only mean he's involved somehow."

"Then . . . then I'll have to delay my own plans and come along," Ian declared.

"Yes. And me, too," Hester stated firmly. "You'll not leave me behind, brother dear."

Her hair in long blond sausage curls, bright eyes twinkling, Hester showed every sign of recovering from her ordeal among the Paiutes and the harrowing escape from the religious fanatics led by Fairgood Hollis. She sat primly in her chair, one slender hand poised over the plate, holding a portion of scrambled eggs on a pewter fork. Her brother's pained expression seemed not to deter her in the least.

"Simple as that. I'm going."

"Now, Hester . . ."

"Ian, I love you dearly and I know I swore to obey you unquestioningly on this journey. In this instance, though, how can I obey you if I'm not with you?"

"Spoken like a lawyer," Lone Wolf chortled.

It earned him a black look from Ian Claymore, who took a short, impatient sip of his coffee. "You, ah, you've managed to outmaneuver me on that point, Hester. All the same . . ."

"I'll not hear anything more on it, Ian. We had better finish our meal and purchase tickets."

Rebecca could not hide the small grin of appreciation that curved her lips. Her only outside sign of approval came in the form of a curt nod.

Early in the morning, the Butterfield stage pulled out of Yuma to take the ferry raft west to the California shore of the Colorado River. There would be two night stops, one at El Centro and the other at Vallecito. The animals would be exchanged three times between each point and twice again during the ascent into the Laguna Mountains. Rebecca and Hester, dressed in traveling clothes, rode in the open-sided mudwagon. Lone Wolf and Ian sat astride handsome Appaloosas, leading the rest of the string of spotted horses.

"We should make mighty good time, least till the sun gets up with a vengeance," their talkative driver informed his passengers.

"Why don't you use the regular Concord coach?" Ian inquired.

"Too heavy. Tires the horses in the heat, and there's soft sand drifts across the roadway. Concord would only bog down. Lest we come on a sudden goose drowner of a rain, these mudwagons are a hull lot more comfortable, too."

Crossing the Colorado became an exhilarating experience. The river's powerful current, masked by a deceptive appearance of placidity, rapidly whisked the hawser-secured flatboat to the extreme limit of the thick, parallel ropes. The slow-moving vehicles of the wagon train had marshaled at the ferry dock, next in line to make the brief voyage. Farewells had been said to Joel and the others. Twelve-year-old Damon Trent hugged Rebecca fiercely and shed a few tears because he could not accompany her. She ruffled his white-blond hair and impulsively kissed him full on the lips.

Damon groaned with a sudden surge of delight and stared glassy-eyed after the coach long after the ferry had made the mile-wide passage to the far shore. "I'll never wash my lips again," he sighed.

"Did she taste real sweet?" Toby Andrews teased.

Damon punched his friend lightly on the chin. "You've got a dirty mind, Toby," he jeered.

On the California riverbank, the coach rolled unsteadily off of the flatboat and the team strained into the harness to haul it up the graded incline. Once on the desert proper, Issac Hughes cracked his long whip over their ears and the six-up of matched bays stretched out into a brisk pace.

"How far did he say it would be to San Diego?" Lone Wolf asked Ian, who rode at his side behind the coach.

"Around a hundred and sixty miles."

"Not so bad, considering the stopover in Julian."

"Right. It'll all be downhill from there. Tell me, Lone Wolf, are you every bit as convinced as Becky is that Roger Styles is behind this Indian trouble?"

"No. Only I've learned to trust her hunches. Either way, we'll know soon enough."

An hour's travel west of the first way station, the coach and outriders came upon a remarkable, eerie sight. For as far as anyone could see, stretched along the roadway, lay an incredible assortment of abandoned objects. Like the Sargasso Sea of housewares and furnishings, the discards of previous travelers rested in single clusters, stacks, and mounds. Eyes bright with excitement, Hester pointed them out.

"Oh, look, Rebecca. Over there. That's an absolutely beautiful fruitwood chiffonier. And there, see that walnut sideboard? Why, these things are priceless. How . . . how did they ever get here?"

"Castoffs, ma'am," Issac called down from the driver's box. "Back 'fore the Mormon Brigade built the plank road, most of the wagons comin' this way were pulled by oxen. The heat and lack of water affected 'em somethin' fierce. As their critters weakened, the folks just pitched off heavy stuff to ease the work that had to be done."

"But . . . so many things. It seems so cruel."

"Folks were sore pressed to decide what to do away with."

Hester rose from the leather-covered seat, holding on to a sidepost of the swaying mudwagon and peering ahead. "There must have been a lot of them. These things look to go on for miles."

"Not as many as you'd think, ma'am. Y'see, the further they went, the harder it became. Ev'ry woman'd hold back those items she most prized in this world. Little by little they had to go, too. Menfolk'd do the same."

"How long ago was this?" Rebecca inquired.

"Oh, say, twenty-five, thirty-five years ago."

"Why haven't these chests and boxes rotted away?" Hester asked.

"Too dry out here. Dry rot and the like's the only thing. Or folks better prepared who come along and pick an' choose from what's here."

"It's . . . all so sad," Hester said softly. "Everything a person most cherished in life. Couldn't we stop and see if there's anything we could take with us to return to some sorrowing mother or child?"

"Not if'n we want to get across this desert without fryin' our brains out," Issac replied curtly.

Ahead now, sparkling whitely in the distance, lay a veritable mountain range of high, impermanent sand dunes. With the horses at a fast trot, it took an endless amount of time for them appear to draw near. Surfeited on the sorrowful view of abandoned dreams, Hester lay back and dozed lightly. Rebecca also closed her eyes and tried to find rest.

A loud rumble awakened both young women. The coach thumped and swayed threatingly, then settled back into the usual movement. The odd noise continued from below the stage. Hester clutched at Rebecca's hand.

"What is it?"

"Look below, Hester. I think you'll see easily enough."

"Why, there's railroad ties under us," Hester exclaimed leaning outward to peer beneath the coach.

"It's the Mormon plank road," Issac's shotgun guard, Manuel Osuna offered. "Since it has been built, travel is much faster and easier to San Diego. Though sometimes we have to stop and shovel sand."

"Why is that?" Hester asked in a distant tone.

Unaware that Manuel Osuna was the grandson of the powerful Osuna family of San Diego County, who owned three of the large Mexican land-grant ranchos, Hester considered the young man to be another menial employee of the stage line. Manuel was looking for adventure and excitement before settling down. He had picked the Butterfield Line as the most likely place to find them. He also found Hester to be attractive, a challenge, like trying to melt ice with sweet words. To reveal this, Manuel reasoned, would be to leave Hester scandalized, so he bided his time until he would woo her with relative hope of success.

"The dunes are constantly shifting, señorita. At no time is the whole of this road free for passage. So," he

42

shrugged with Latin eloquence, "we must keep busy to clear the way."

"Is it always this noisy?"

"Only when the wind has blown the planks free of all sand, señorita."

Flashing a big, white smile, the handsome youth laid aside his shotgun and swung low over the side of the coach. With his free hand he offered a canteen of water.

"Have something to drink, señorita. It is another two hours to the next way station."

"Why, uh, uh . . ."

"Go ahead," Rebecca whispered to her. "Take it. Or go thirsty."

Hester's condescending attitude toward the stage driver and guard had begun to irritate Rebecca. This was a side of the former captive girl she had not seen before. She resolved to do what she could to bring a change of heart.

For all her hardness and determination, her willingness to kill like a man in a man's world, Rebecca loved romance. Her own or that of others. The poems of that delightful young Miss Elizabeth Barrett of London made tears come to her eyes. The idea of amorous sparks being struck between Hester and Manuel made her romantic soul soar. She would definitely, she firmly promised herself, see what could be done.

"Half-hour dinner stop at the next way station," Issac called out.

After a meal of *frijoles, tortillas, arroz con pollo*, and coffee, the coach started out again. Two hours along the trail, everything went well, the speedy mudwagon making good time along the plank road.

An explosive crack sounded and sections of two stout oak spokes flew outward from one wheel. Immediately Issac began to rein in the six-up.

"Whoa! Whoa-up there, you critters. Easy Belle, Ned, Rufus. Whoa."

The violent noise once more awakened a drowsing Hester Claymore. "What is it? What happened?"

"Awh, hell an' tarnation . . . er, yer pardon ma'am, the danged wheel threw a couple spokes. We're gonna be stuck here fer a spell whilst I changes off. Everybody out."

"Stuck here? In the middle of nothing? Whatever shall we do?"

Rebecca took Hester aside. "For starters, you might listen to a bit of exciting news I've learned."

"What's that?"

"You know that handsome, clean-faced young man who is our shotgun guard?"

"Oh, him. What about him?"

"He's actually the grandson of some very wealthy land-grant holders in this county. He has a fantastic place of his own and is quite rich. He guards the stages for excitement."

"Oh, you're making fun of me, Rebecca."

"No, I'm not. Go ask him if his full name is Manuel Osuna."

Hester's gaze shifted to where Manuel aided Issac in setting up the step jack to raise the rear axel. Rebecca could read the heightening interest as the girl took her first close examination of the good-looking young man. Perhaps she'd managed to start something after all, she congratulated herself.

Chapter 5

Of medium height, though lean and athletically youthful, Frank Kimball strode briskly down Main Street in San Diego toward the offices of the Horton Development Company. Gulls circled and screeched above. A salt tang hung heavy in the air. Kimball nodded at acquaintances and never failed to doff his hat respectfully to the ladies. The silver head on his blackthorn cane gleamed in the watery sunlight. When he reached his destination, he paused only a fraction of a second before turning the large brass knob and entering.

"Good morning, Mr. Kimball," the prim, pinch-faced male secretary greeted him.

"Morning, Jasper. Mr. Horton is expecting me."

"Yes, sir. Go right in."

Alonzo Horton rose to greet his visitor. As they shook hands, Horton waved negligently toward the large accumulation of papers on the flat surface of his rolltop desk.

"There never seems to be an end to it. How are you, Frank?"

"Troubled, to put it mildly."

Horton's genial expression altered to one of sincere concern. "Oh? What seems to be the matter?"

"That crass lout you steered into optioning Vladimir's holdings in South Bay. Already he's infringing on land that belongs to Rancho de la Nación. Like you, I thought that ground between our property and Rancho Otay would be enough to satisfy his ambitions. Apparently not. I'm trying to build a city and he's trying to steal it right out from under me. My brothers are really hot over this. They decided to go over there and settle matters. It didn't work out so good."

"I agree, Roger Styles is greedy and far from diplomatic. His dealings with Count Vladimir were, ah . . . unctious is too polite . . . just plain oily best describes his maneuverings. What happened when your brothers confronted him?"

"They didn't. Styles wasn't there. He went off somewhere, 'looking for land to buy,' according to the scruffy underling he'd left behind. This particular individual, and three others, displayed firearms and literally forced my brothers off the property."

"Oh, my, that is becoming serious."

"There's worse to tell. Did you know that Styles has surrounded himself with a band of nearly seventy wharf rats and riffraff from the waterfront? He's armed them, for God's sake. For whatever reason, I can't surmise."

Alonzo Horton considered this revelation a moment. "Perhaps . . . we should all take a hand in this. I've heard, ah, disturbing reports from the back country. Nothing too unusual, actually. Bandits do raid the Indians from time to time. It's regrettable, but it's the Army's job to protect them. I wish Sheriff Hunsaker had more authority in such matters. Slavers. These bandits are little more than that. They kill off any who resist, take the older boys and young women off to Mexico."

"I know," Frank Kimball responded. "I've also written to our senators asking that jurisdiction over the Indian reservations to be given to the county sheriff. So far, Washington does nothing, as usual. In the meantime, we still have Roger Styles to deal with."

"Right you are, Frank. I'll call a meeting for tomorrow night, at my house. Drinks at seven? Dinner at eight-thirty. After that we can decide."

"Thank you, Alonzo. I knew we'd have to go into this with mutual commitment. Damnit, that man is dangerous."

Heat waves shimmered off the stark white dunes. Some distance from where Rebecca Caldwell shaded herself under a low smoke tree, a pale, tan-white snake made its tortuous way across the burning sand in an ungainly sideways motion. Disturbed by the thumps and bangs of the repair work, its evil temper aroused by other unwanted vibrations, the sidewinder had violated its life-preserving habit of seclusion during the heat of day to get retribution. At that moment, the object of its revenge was Hestor Claymore.

The barely audible cessation of the snake's progress across the fine-grained sand alerted Rebecca to some unidentified danger. She scanned the area, expecting to see some person or animal stalking them. Her dark blue eyes nearly missed the sensuous articulation of the deadly viper. When she recognized it, the reptile had closed with its intended victim to the point where a shouted warning could bring disaster. Swiftly, Rebecca dipped her right hand into the voluminous velvet purse she held in her lap. With equal speed, she withdrew it.

Crack!

Her single shot shounded shatteringly loud in the desert stillness. Hester squeaked in fright and the men's voices blared out in startled query. The sidewinder thrashed on the sand, headless, spewing out its life force.

"Snake," Rebecca said blandly. "It was going for Hester."

"Jingoes, ma'am!" Issac Hughes exclaimed as he hurried up. "I had no idee you was packin' iron. Let alone that you could shoot so good."

"We live in strange times, Mr. Hughes," Rebecca responded in a tone of amusement.

"Call me Ike, Miss . . . ah . . ."

"Rebecca," the lovely young woman supplied. "How much longer, Ike?"

"We only got to slip on the spare and cinch down the hub nut. Say . . . ten minutes."

"Wonderful."

"We'll make El Centro a mite late, Miss Rebecca, but we'll get there."

Issac Hughes bent low over the step jack lever to lower the rear axel. He had just begun to bob up and down when Rebecca noticed a fleeting suggestion of movement beyond the nearest dune. Windblown sand? It was possible. Only it could also have been dust thrown up by the hooves of several horses. A moment later, two men in wide-brimmed, silver-thread-decorated hats, the scoop edges turned upward in a rakish manner, appeared over the rise. They sat their horses and studied the people below. The white squaw's keen eyesight enabled her to observe their brief discussion. When they reached agreement, they immediately acted upon it.

With one accord, the pair rode down the shifting slope toward the stagecoach. When they came within hailing distance the men halted, and the taller, thinner of them raised his hand.

"*Buenas tardes,*" he greeted.

"*Muy buenas,*" Manuel replied.

"*Tienenos problemas?*"

"*Sí*. But we have taken care of it now," Manuel

continued in Spanish. "It was a broken wheel."

"*Muy malo, chico.* We heard a shot. That is what brought us here."

"A sidewinder, tried to bite the pretty señorita."

"*Ay, muy mal fortuna. Tien cuidado, bonita.* You are going to El Centro?"

"*Sí.* What else does the Yuma stage do, señores?"

"Ah-hah! You make the joke, no? That is good. We are *vaqueros* on our way to San Cristobol in Sonora, so we wish you well. *Adios, señores, señoras.*"

"*Vaya con dios,*" Manuel replied.

When the men had departed, the young Mexican spat on the ground. "*Bandidos chingados!*" he cursed.

"What is it, Manuel?" Hester inquired, eyes wide with concern.

"They are not *vaqueros* on their way to San Cristobol. They are bandits. Had we been fewer in number, or less well armed, they would have robbed us."

"Oh, my! A-are we safe now?"

"I would say so. Too many guns for the liking of those scum."

"Load up, everybody," Issac Hughes called out. "We're off to El Centro."

Muffled by the sand, the hoofbeats of a dozen horses could not be heard until the scruffy bandits crested the nearest dune and pushed downward on the stage. Hester had entered the coach, leaving Rebecca and the others outside. Issac glanced up and pointed, one hand going for the model '68 Winchester beside him on the seat.

"Damn! There's more of 'em. Bandits comin' our way," he called out.

Manuel grabbed for his shotgun and took cover on the far side of the coach. Lone Wolf and Ian Claymore spread apart, intent on keeping the advantage of mounted men in a swiftly moving battle.

49

"*Los manos arriba!*" Rudolfo Mateo shouted from the center of the charging line.

Rather than put up their hands as instructed, Manuel yelled back defiantly, "*Chinga tu madre!*"

To enforce his incestuous suggestion, he sent along a load of double-aught buckshot, which slashed the horse out from under the man next to Mateo. Shrieking in agony, the plunging animal went down in the forelegs and hurtled its rider over its head.

"*Cabrón!* I shall roast your *cojones* for this!" Mateo bellowed. At his signal, rifles and six-guns opened up among the bandits.

"It's not my balls that will roast, *hijo de tu madre!*" Manuel taunted back.

Ian and Lone Wolf opened fire from the flanks. Rebecca, who had joined Manuel and Issac on the far side of the coach, unlimbered one of her horse pistols, a .44 Smith and Wesson American. She had taken it from the brace of revolvers inside the coach. Determinedly she eared back the hammer. A bandit filled all the frame of the opposite side of the mudwagon. Hester quivered in apprehension only scant inches from his grasp. Rebecca squeezed the trigger.

Orange flame and dirty-white smoke spewed from the barrel of the .44, while the heavy 210-grain slug sped toward the bright concho that twinkled on the left breast of the bandit's shirt. Lead struck silver and the Mexican outlaw catapulted backward off his horse.

"Grab up that other six-gun," Rebecca yelled at Hester. "I haven't time to defend you and me, too."

The volume of fire increased on the flanks. Men cried out in pain and surprise. Gradually the bandits pulled back from their objective. Rebecca blasted off two more rounds at the dark forms amid churning sand dust. One of her bullets punched a neat hole in the brim of Mateo's charro sombrero.

"Oye muchachos, andale. Vaminos!"

In scant seconds, the surviving bandits pulled off from the attack and rode to safety behind the shifting dunes. *"Una mujer!"* Rudolfo Mateo spat in disgust when he reined in.

"Did you see her? *Ella se cree la divina garza!"*

"Ay, sí. Hot stuff indeed, Rudolfo," one of his followers jeered. "She damn near blew off your head."

"Mierda! Algun dia yo se vengara de elle. Yes," Rudolfo repeated, eyes blazing with fury, "I'll get even with her someday."

"They've gone," Hester gasped out with relief.

"Pero no," Manuel began, then switched to English. "But not necessarily for good."

"You've got it, Manny. We'd better get this rig rollin'," Issac suggested, climbing to the driver's box.

Long, purple shadows lay on the red-brown desert soil, the sun far over toward the western mountains, when the mudwagon coach rolled up before the Butterfield Stage Line station in El Centro. Outside the steeples of two churches, the building was the tallest in town. The lower floor, made of adobe blocks, had been there before the coming of the stage service. The upper, which provided barracks facilities for the permanent employees and overnight accommodations for passengers, had been added later.

Constructed of board-and-batt siding, the second story had but three windows on a side and the entire structure leaked sand constantly. To Rebecca's eyes, El Centro seemed more an abandoned mining camp than a town struggling to grow. A few half-naked children, mostly of mixed Anglo, Mexican, and Indian origins, raced alongside the stage, shrilling in high-pitched voices, their bare feet raising puffs of dust. Old men with white mustaches, their large straw sombreros pushed low over their eyes, slept on benches in front of the saloons. A few horses stood, hip-shot, at tie-rails, indicating that the village might come alive with the cooling air. None of it looked entirely inviting.

"El Centro!" Issac called out. "Night stop. Ev'rbody out. Take ev'r'thing ya've got, so's it'll be here in the mornin'. There's food inside."

Once the ladies had disembarked, followed by two gentlemen who had boarded at the last way station, Issac stepped closer to Rebecca and Hester. "There's food available, right enough. But there's also three cafes in town. I'd advise any one of them over the grub here. Ev'r since our Chinee cook took the fever and died, it's been lousy vittles."

"Why, thank you, Ike."

Hughes grinned like a love-struck boy. "Yer welcome, Miss Rebecca."

Rebecca, Lone Wolf, Ian, and Hester took Issac's advice. They chose the second restaurant they inspected, because of the savory aromas that wafted out into the night air rather than because of the menu. Written in chalk on a wooden bound slate, the Spanish language bill of fare stood upright on a porch roof.

MENU

10¢   COMIDA CORRIDA   10¢

Carnitas de Puerco

Carne con Chili Colorado

Enchiladas Verde

(*Caldo, Sopa Seca, Frijoles, Aroz, encl.*)

Sopa de la Tarde: Cuahuama

Pescado Fresco Viernes y Sabado solomente.

¡Tome Cerveza TECETE!

To her delight, Rebecca found the *carnitas de puerco* to

be bits of pork, cooked in large chunks in a giant copper cauldron over a manzanita wood fire and seasoned with the potent Mexican liquor, tequila. A large mound of the tender brown morsels came with a condiment tray from which she selected a variety to roll into fresh-baked tortillas along with the meat. She enjoyed every bite. Lone Wolf had the *carne con chili colorado*, which turned out to be stew-sized hunks of beef, simmered in a blistering gravy of tomatoes, onions, and red chili pepper pods, which nearly dissolved the roof of his mouth. He chewed, sweated, and savored every morsel. Ian suggested the green chili enchiladas for Hester, who complained even so about the spicy nature of the food. He opted for *carnitas*, which he savored every bit as much as Rebecca. They washed it all down with draughts of tepid beer.

Fully sated, filled to overflowing, they returned to the Butterfield Stage hostelry and retired for the night. The excitement of the bandit attack, which had been the sole topic of conversation in town that evening, combined with the long hours on the road in desert heat quickly took their toll.

Paramount in Rebecca's mind was the fact they had two more difficult days to go before reaching the cool mountains far to the west.

Chapter 6

Fear had been added to oppression in the hearts of the Indians of San Diego County. The impudent jays still scolded from the tops of the oaks. The ground squirrels and rabbits continued to frisk about the land. Bright cardinals added flashes of scarlet as they streaked through the air. The sun rose and set, winds blew, hot or cold. The rains came, colder all the time. Snow capped the higher peaks of the Laguna Mountains. And DEATH stalked the valleys and canyons. Every day, more Diegueño and Cahuilla people became victims of horrible murders and mutilations.

There were some, at Barona and other reservations, who felt that they should take action to stop the butchery of their people. Only in the earliest days of the Spanish invasion, the elders reminded the younger, hotter-headed ones, had the residents of this region put up any resistance. At a large meeting held by the people of Barron Long—or Barona, as the outsiders had chosen to call it—these tales of valor were recounted.

"Hair Pipe came down with all the warriors from above the Pala Valley. Quietly they stole in among the horses and mules of the Steel Hats at the Presidio of San Diego. Small boys led the animals away," recounted grizzled old Ewi. "These steeds were taken in turn by warriors of this high grass valley. While the

Steel Hats slept, our people crept in among them and cut their throats. One man, who the grandfathers tell us was named Xeliau, did this work badly. The one he was supposed to dispatch did not die. Rather he cried out in horror and pain.

"It aroused the camp of the Steel Hats. A great clangor came from an iron hoop outside the mud and log building. It awakened the Black Robes before they could be dispatched by other warriors. The Steel Hats began to use their fire-weapons. Many true-men died. Boys of the true-people died also that night. The Black Robes chanted and made magical gestures, all the while armed with the long knives of the *Española*. Our people were forced to retreat.

"When the Sky Father returned the next day," Ewi went on, wiping a thin tendril of spittle from one corner of his toothless mouth. He sighed before he advanced the tale. "When Sky Father returned, all who could do so had fled up the course of the river toward Sun Meadow—the valley since called El Cajon. The wounded, and those who had surrendered, had been gathered by the Steel Hats. A great council was held by the Black Robes and the chief of the Steel Hats. Men of their kind brought out ropes and tossed them over the limbs of stout oaks. Others built boxes upon which our warriors would be made to stand. Crossbars above these boxes also supported ropes."

Ancient Rattlesnake stopped his narrative for a long while. He drank of a fermented beverage made of wild honey, fanned himself with a hawk wing, shook his head and sighed. When he spoke again, it was in a sing-song rhythm, his tone one of a lament.

"The captives were brought forth from the building called *el cabildo*. First they were scourged with a whip. Those who would recant were given a chance to do so. To the shame of our people, many did. They were

55

branded upon their thumbs, put into wooden yokes about their necks and set to work at the new mission being built up the river valley. As to the others, their fate was not so shameful, but still lacked honor. They were dragged to the trees and boxes and stood in place. Loops of rope were fitted over their heads and they were pulled into the air to die in dishonor and degradation. All this, said the Black Robes, for the greater glory of God and *El Rey de España*."

"Was nothing done to revenge this?" young Juan Lachusa asked earnestly.

"We fought several times after this. Some of the Black Robes died. Some of the Steel Hats gave up their lives. More of our people failed to return from each battle. While our numbers decreased, theirs increased. There seemed no end to them. So, the grandfathers of old decided it would not be wise to continue to anger them. One last fight was agreed upon. At the mission in the valley. The Steel Hats came swiftly on horses, even while the outbuildings burned and the slaves ran free. The Steel Hats brought with them the long gun that speaks far away. More of our warriors met the Other World."

Ewi ceased and his chin sank onto his emaciated chest. "In the end, our people knew bitter defeat. There would be no more wars against the Spanish, or any other conquerors who came after them."

"But what of now?" several anxious voices called out.

"These things aren't the doings of those who have taken our land. Not soldiers or priests. They can die. We have killed them," another Diegueño warrior declared. "So have our brothers and the Cahuilla. Here is Victor Occatillo come from the Warner's Springs people. He says many of the Cahuilla have died, too. Those who attack us wear no uniforms, bring no long shoot guns. They're renegades among their own kind.

Bandits. We can, we must, fight them."

"*Ekwi-'etru,*" Rattlesnake said chidingly, "you are too eager to shed blood. Don't you see that it will most likely be the blood of the Diegueño?"

"Better it be shed in battle," Victor Occatillo snarled, "than on one's sleeping robes."

For a moment, Cloud Belly glowered at Ewi. "My family is gone. All of them. My boy-children are taken off to be slaves. Now our people die for no reason, their hair cut off in some disgusting manner of the *xaiqu.* Yet, you say there is nothing we can do? *I* can do something. *I* can kill *xaiqu,* make them bleed, make them run in terror. *I* can do it . . . and so can we all! Kill the *xaiqu!* Strike fear into their hearts! Drive them from our mountains."

In the passion of the moment, all tribal rivalries had been put aside. Victor Occatillo and his twenty-four Cahuilla warriors had been welcomed like brothers, feasted and allowed to partake in this council. Now Victor stepped forward, his sardonic features flickeringly illuminated by the bonfire. He spoke with the freedom of a tribesman.

"Until the flood of strange white men began, our people and yours had gotten along well enough, if not ideally, with the Spanish and the Mexicans. After the bad times in the first days of their coming, a way of life remained to us. Then came the true *xaiqu,* out of the East, their pale skins and greedy hands an offense to all who knew and lived in this land. We must band together to drive the whites out of the mountains and off the desert and away from the shores of the Big Water. Not only those responsible for the killings and burning, but all *xaiqu!* All must be removed from our land."

"No!" Juan Lachusa objected. "This is not wise. It is not possible. Surely as the Spanish came in ever-increasing numbers, so the *xaiqu* from beyond the Colorado River will do. If one falls, ten will rise to take his place. I would rather seek the help of the honest ones among their kind to catch the evildoers."

"You were raised in the mission school, Juan," Victor sneered. "You have given your heart to their *Kuyaho-mar*, Jesus. You have served them like a dog by holding their horses. You have wet your *meri* in the bodies of whites. If you have any balls, you have given them over to the safekeeping of the *xaiqu*. You have become our *esann*," he ended in a disgusted snarl.

"*Kosmirai-ly!*" Juan shouted back. "Yes, you are crazy. Mad with the lust to draw blood. I don't want to fight you, Victor Occatillo. Enough of the blood of our two people has been shed already. I only say we should look further into this. Find out by whom and why it's being done. Then strike. If I'm but your little sister, then let the women lead. At least until we know who our enemy is. Then we can all wash our knives in *xaiqu* blood."

"The time to start is now," Victor insisted. "Before more of these evil ones can enter our land, we must close it off. We will begin with the *xaiqu* in the wagons that bring more of their kind. We will begin with the next sun!"

Hearty shouts of agreement answered him.

So far, considering the violent confrontation of the previous afternoon, the day had gone uneventfully. The two men who had boarded the stage after the set-to with bandits identified themselves as Basque sheep ranchers. Conversation became less strained during the peaceful journey between El Centro and Vallicito.

"Oh, yes, long ago our people come from Spain."

"You're Spanish, then, Mr. Vegas?" Hester inquired.

Vegas frowned slightly. "No. Not exactly. The

Basque country lies in an area of the Pyrenees Mountains, part in Spain, part in France. Our Basque people consider themselves to be of neither nationality. But we have always been raisers of sheep and oxen. The best in all the world," the dark-complected man ended proudly.

"You mentioned bringing your flocks to the desert for the winter," Rebecca inserted. "Where had they been during the hottest part of the year?"

"Why, up in the mountains. There are springs and rich meadows around the small Basque town of Jacumba. Our flocks do well there. It's a strange place, Jacumba."

"How's that?"

"Half of each year there's hardly anyone living there. When the flocks are down here, the people go with them. Jacumba has mineral springs, like the fancy spas of Europe. So the summer months are sort of a long festival for us. Though, I personally enjoy the desert."

Hester made a face. "There are dangerous snakes out here."

Vegas shrugged. "There are three varieties of rattlesnake in the mountains. We're used to them. Our flocks grow larger all the time."

A natural salesman, Vegas's companion, Macuerez, leaned forward. "We're going to San Diego to open a new market for our wool and lambs. It's a growing town and in need of a fresh supply of meat. Also, the price for wool should be higher than trading with the Mexicans at Mexicali."

"Anton is the business head for our community," Vegas explained. "He's always looking out for what's best. I agree with him, though, that San Diego holds a lot of promise for us. It's only that the distance is so great."

"Fifteen miles to Vallecito," Issac called out to his

passengers. "We'll be there in a bit less than two hours."

"I must say I feel grateful that we've been spared an experience such as you encountered yesterday," Vegas declared. "Bandits are a terrible nuisance."

"Don't they ever bother your sheep, Mr. Vegas?" Hester asked.

"No, not to any great extent. Sometimes they take a sheep or two, but mostly they leave us alone. I think they consider shepherds too poor to bother to rob."

Issac's forecast proved accurate. The Butterfield coach arrived at the low, sprawling adobe structure that formed the Vallecito stage station fifteen minutes short of two hours later. A gnarled-handed, stooped old man freed the trace chains and led the lathered team away to a corral, while Issac and Manuel assisted the passengers in dismounting.

"You can leave yer belongin's in the boot if ya like. Nobody around here to steal anything," he informed them.

Lone Wolf and Ian Claymore tended to their mounts and the spare animals, then joined the others on a roofed-over verandah to watch a spectacular sunset over the purple mountains. From this close, the Laguna range appeared to be an impenetrable wall erected between the desert and the seacoast.

"We're going up those in the morning," Lone Wolf observed. "Wouldn't surprise me if you ladies had to get out and push."

"The road is a good one," Vegas assured them. "You'll be going up to Julian. The express coach takes the Mormon Road through Jacumba, to Campo and straight into San Diego. It's faster, though naturally more uncomfortable."

"The colors are so spectacular here on the desert," Hester exclaimed, transported by the rich mixture of pastel blues, pinks, and violets, blended with deep rust-browns and long purple shadows.

"It is . . . why I prefer this land to the mountains," Vegas replied somewhat shyly.

"Why, Mr. Vegas," Hester responded coyly, "I believe you have the soul of a poet."

Following a remarkably excellent supper of *cabrito*, which Hester declared to be the best roast pork she had ever eaten, having been kept blissfully ignorant that the meat was in fact roast goat, Rebecca and Ian took a casual stroll around the grounds of the stage stop. The barn seemed to invite them, so they walked nearer.

A ramshackle building, the structure had been built, like the station, partly underground. It provided cooler stalls for animals housed there. The foreshortened upper portion could thus be entered by climbing four stout steps from ground level.

Inside, the tingling sweet odor of decomposing hay tantalized their nostrils. Despite the lack of light, Rebecca's eyes sparkled. Ian sensed her heightened ardor and placed an arm around her shoulders. She laid her head on his chest.

"It's so peaceful here. No wonder Vegas loves the desert." Rebecca murmured. "I feel so . . ."

"Wanton?" Ian asked her urgently. A familiar heat had kindled in his loins as he responded to her mood.

"Wha . . . well, if I think on it a little . . . yes. I feel incredibly wanton. Can we find a place there, where we can be alone?"

"I'm sure we can." Ian released her and they bent low, searching for an open place or some fresher hay.

"Over here," Rebecca called out. "I've found a delightful spot."

Someone had gone to considerable effort. Hay had been moved around, to form a roughly circular cove in the high stack. A blanket had been laid over it, to provide comfort. A shaft of moonlight faintly illumi-

61

nated the place and revealed several toys. No doubt some of the many children who swarmed around the stage station had designed this as a hideout.

"Oh, Ian. I think it's charming."

"Yes, it is. It's . . . perfect."

Ian took her in his arms and they kissed with growing desire. Rebecca thrilled to the strength and closeness of the tall, broad-chested young man. Her pulse raced as his tongue probed at the inside of her mouth. She felt a wave of weakness pass through her body, to be replaced by the raging fires of lust. One hand slid between their closely fitted bodies and sought out the swollen evidence of his passion.

Gently she squeezed the rigid projection that strained against the material of Ian's trousers. She moaned and began purposefully to stroke him. Their embrace ended and Rebecca knelt before him. Quickly, expertly, she opened his fly and extracted his throbbing, shaft. Her fingers played a tantalizing rhythm and Ian muttered in appreciation. Long, black hair slithered down to hide Rebecca's lovely profile when she bent her head forward.

Warm, moist lips closed over Ian's burning flesh. With consummate skill, Rebecca plied lips, tongue and fingers to send powerful surges of pleasure through his fevered body. She trembled with her own excitement and increased the bobbing movement of her upper body.

"Aaah. Gently, gently, love," Ian cautioned. "No need to end this all too soon."

Rebecca paced herself. Her heart pounded and she ached to give her utmost. Even so, she resorted to a slow, gentle, excruciatingly wonderful cadence that proclaimed the depths of her affection for the man she served so dilligently. Ian expressed his appreciation and gratitude in the manner in which he touched her lightly here and there. Slowly the inevitable came upon him and he joyfully went over the peak.

Long moments passed before Rebecca disengaged herself from Ian's body. When she did, the impassioned pair swiftly removed their clothing and lay side by side on the blanket. Ian's long, experienced fingers began to explore Rebecca's silken figure, gliding over the warm flesh, finding new places to stimulate her, reducing her former inner calm to quaking confusion.

"Ummmm. You're so good for me," Rebecca crooned.

"And you make any day brighter. We're good together, Becky."

"Thank you, kind sir. Now, there's something important to be done."

For her own part, Rebecca paid careful attention to once again arousing Ian's muscular flesh. In the throes of wildest abandon, Rebecca drew her lover to her.

Rocking with shallow, rapid thrusts, Ian slowly entered her feverish body. He maintained his teasing, taunting penetration until fully encased in her musk-sweet flesh. Then he began to plunge with determination.

"Oh . . . oh, Ian. Yes, yes, yes. Harder, oh, yes. Aaaah! Aaaaah!"

Rebecca knew no greater happiness. She strained to give every bit as much as she received. Time halted on the brink of a chasm, poised to tumble over. White-hot, her mind went into a whirl, leaving Roger Styles, the jail at Yuma, and everything else far, far away.

Long into the night, she and Ian strived mutually to keep the harsher aspects of reality at bay. For the most part, they most ecstatically succeeded.

Chapter 7

High above, in the topmost branches of the pines, a warm, dry northeast wind moaned. Dubbed a *santana* by the Spanish-speaking residents of San Diego County, the heated air would bring temperatures of near one hundred degrees to the inland valleys. Sixty feet below, on the ground near Cuyamaca Mountain, hardly a breeze stirred. Gray and red-brown squirrels chased through the branches, unmindful that winter was only a short time away. Chipmunks chittered noisily and went about storing away seed pods and acorns for the sparse time that drew near. Frivolous insects buzzed about, iridescent wings catching the stark brightness of a clear, warming sun. In so tranquil a scene, it seemed impossible that deadly menace lurked for the unsuspecting.

Victor Occatillo nodded in satisfaction as he listened to the report. His scouts had done well. Soon now he, and the warriors with him, would taste revenge for the many slain by the white men.

"You've done well, Pablo. We'll gather at the place where the trail is steepest. None of them shall escape." He turned to Xawok Axat, his Diegueño counterpart, and issued terse orders.

Two Dogs smiled grimly, pleased with the prospect of victory as outlined by his Cahuilla cousin. They would indeed make the *xaiqu* pay for the lives lost.

Rattling and bouncing along, a sheer drop of from four hundred to a thousand feet on the left side, the Butterfield coach labored into the ascent of the eastern face of the Laguna Mountains. Señor Vegas and his companion, Macuerez, had remained at Vallecito to take the express coach through the newer, secondary route to San Diego. That left Rebecca Caldwell and Hester Claymore alone in the mudwagon. Over the clatter of the journey they tried to carry on a conversation.

"Do you think he could really take an interest in me?" Hester asked in a lowered voice.

"Who, dear?" Rebecca returned in an innocent tone belied by the twinkle in her deep blue eyes.

"Manuel, of course!" Hester snapped, irritated by this sudden switch in Rebecca's earlier stand. "He *is* handsome, like you pointed out. And he was so brave when the bandits attacked us."

"Do I detect a positive change in your outlook, Hester?"

The young Kentucky girl blushed. "You're teasing me."

"Of course I am. You'd have to be blind not to see how Manuel feels toward you. All you have to do is . . . offer a little something."

"Like what? You don't mean . . . ?"

"No. Certainly not at this stage. Smile. Flirt with him a little. Flatter him. All those little things that the Eastern ladies call 'feminine wiles.' You haven't much time, you know. Once the stage reaches San Diego, you may never see him again."

"Oh! I . . . never thought of it that way. Can you

. . . would you . . . help me?"

"Whatever could I do that you couldn't do better? You're young, healthy, attractive. He's handsome and definitely enamored of the ladies. We have one more stop, at the top of the grade, then Julian for overnight. Make the best of the time you have."

"Oh, Rebecca, thank you for clearing my thoughts."

Hester started to lean forward to hug the young woman who sat opposite her. As she did, an arrow whizzed past, between them. Hester recoiled with a piercing shriek.

"What was that?"

"An arrow," Rebecca answered in a sensible tone as she bent to the carpet bag that held her gunbelt.

Gunshots sounded from the uphill side of the coach. Three arrows thudded into the low wooden sides. Issac slapped the reins on the rumps of his team and called to them to pull harder.

"Injuns, fer God's sake!" the grizzled driver shouted. "I don't believe it."

"They're real enough, *amigo*," Manuel answered calmly.

Behind the coach, Lone Wolf and Ian drew their sidearms and blasted shots into the thick, screening brush. The former Crow warrior pointed slightly ahead of the plunging six-up of lathered horses.

"There. See the movement. Looks like they're going to try to block the road. Concentrate on that spot. I'll cover our rear."

Ian's long-barreled six-gun barked loudly and the slug gouged a shower of bark shards from a resin-glistening pine. The sharp-edged bits cut small slashes on Two Dogs's face. A warrior close to him groaned softly and dug at the brown material that filled his eyes. Claymore fired again, a moment after Lone Wolf. The warriors drew back into the protecting screen of

66

trees. Manuel's shotgun erupted with smoke and flame. Double-aught pellets slashed the foliage and ripped into bronze flesh behind. Lone Wolf holstered his six-gun and drew the heavy Sharps from its saddle scabbard. He took aim on a red-brown form that ran toward the roadway behind them. The .50-caliber buffalo gun roared and a Cahuilla flew backward as though on a giant spring.

"Use your rifle, Ian, we need all the accuracy we can get. Otherwise they'll be right on top of us."

Claymore complied, sliding his Remington revolver into the waistband of his trousers and drawing a Winchester. Three figures leaped onto the road ahead of the coach, waving blankets at the wall-eyed horses. Ian took careful aim and shot the one in the center.

Blood flew from the Cahuilla warrior's back as the .44-40 slug smashed through the chest and sheered away part of one vertebra. He spun slowly to his left and fell in the decomposed granite that formed the trail bed. Ian worked the lever again and sighted on another attacker. From inside the coach, Rebecca's Smith American spoke with deep-throated authority. Manuel lay flat on the top of the coach, firing at any sensed movement. Issac cried out suddenly and clutched at the inside surface of his right thigh. The crude shaft and fletchings of a Diegueño arrow twitched and wobbled between his fingers.

"Yer gonna have to drive, Manny, while I get this danged thing out," Issac told his shotgun guard.

Manuel emptied both barrels in rapid succession and slid back on the seat. He took the reins in one hand, the whip in the other. With both he lashed at the horses, urging more speed. Issac snapped off the arrow some three inches above his skin. With a curse he flung it away, then reached for the razor-honed knife at this side.

"This ain't gonna be too easy," he muttered. "Sure could use a stiff shot of whiskey."

"You can have it after we get outta here," Manuel offered grimly.

The improvised roadblock had been successfully passed now. Lone Wolf spotted a fairly open meadow ahead. He pointed it out to Ian Claymore.

"Let's cut through there, flank 'em and hit them in the rear."

"Good idea. Sure wish I had some of those bombs we used on the Paiutes."

"Too close. We'd get it as bad as them."

Ian sighed. "You're right, of course. What about the coach and the ladies?"

"Rebecca can take care of that. She and Manuel."

Issac had taken back the reins after he found the lurching platform too unstable for him to safely carve on his leg. Manuel reloaded the ten-gauge Parker and once more sought targets of opportunity. The yipping, howling Indians soon gave him plenty. He blasted two into eternity with a single charge. Lone Wolf and Ian swung away from the roadway at that moment and Manuel tapped Issac on the shoulder.

"Where are they goin', Ike?"

"Get around behind 'em, I'd say," the older man responded. "Damnit, this things smarts a mite."

From inside the coach, Rebecca's voice came calm and assuring. "Keep down, Hester. You'll be all right."

Her Smith American spoke again and a Cahuilla warrior howled in pain as his left elbow shattered. A staccato burst of gunfire from behind the ambushers verified Issac's estimation of Lone Wolf's plan. A moment later, Rebecca sensed a lessening of intensity in the battle. There came more shouts of defiance and less firing from the hidden warriors. More shots racketed off the face of the mountain from the enemy's rear, and then a commanding voice called loudly.

"Run, get away. Back through the canyon," Victor Occatillo ordered.

With a suddenness more shattering than its commencement, the fighting ended.

Lone Wolf and Ian Claymore appeared on the road, behind the laboring coach. A wave of Lone Wolf's arm indicated that the enemy had fled the field. Issac reined in the frothing-mouthed team.

"Now, for certain sure, I've gotta dig out that arrowhead," he declared.

"Best wait until we get to the way station," Manuel suggested.

Issac grimaced. "Yer right, of course."

"Will they be back?" Hester asked timidly.

"I doubt it," Rebecca answered.

"You can't count on that," Issac remarked from the driver's box. "It's danged unusual them particular Injuns attacked at all. There hasn't been any Injun trouble in these parts fer so long nobody can recall it. In fact, the Diegueños are reckoned to be so back'ard, and so cowed by the Spanish mission system that had 'em in their tender clutches for so long, that they never knew how to go to war."

"So what caused this, Ike?" Rebecca inquired.

"I don't know, Miss Rebecca. I plain don't have a handle on it."

"I'd like to know more about it," Rebecca speculated aloud. "We heard reports that the Indians were being victimized. Could they . . . would they think of retaliating?"

"Why'd they pick on us if they did?" Issac summed it up for all of them.

When the door to his small office flew open with enough force to cause it to rebound off the inner wall,

Roger Styles cleared his chair by a good two inches in a startled reaction. Immediately he tried to gather his scattered thoughts. In the opening stood Alonzo Horton. The entrepeneur didn't look at all cordial.

"I, uh, daresay, Alonzo. That's hardly a, ah, friendly way to pay a visit."

"There's nothing 'friendly' about this visit, *Mister* Styles."

"Why, what do you mean?"

"This gentleman with me . . ." Horton stepped aside to allow another man to enter the officer. "This is Sheriff Hunsaker. He's been getting reports of murders and mutilations among the Indians in the back country. I have a strong feeling you could enlighten us as to why this is going on."

Although pierced by an icy bolt of fear, Roger kept his expression bland and shrugged casually. "I don't see how I could. Indians are Indians. They're just doing what comes naturally."

"It's not intertribal warfare. There have been a few survivors. They claim that white men are attacking them."

"It must be bandits, then. Vladimir told me about the Mexican slavers who raid across the border from Baja California. There, it's simple as that."

Horton scowled and the sheriff took a step forward before he spoke. Hunsaker's voice came out like the rusty hinges of a mausoleum.

"The Indians around here call Mexicans Mexicans. In these incidents, they used the word *xaiqo*. That means *white men*, Anglos, men like the kind of scum you've been hiring lately."

"Have you . . . have you anything more to say?" Roger asked, his throat tight.

"Yes," Horton replied. "But we'll come to that in a moment. First, let me ask you this. Do you have any idea what happens to lands currently being held in trust for the Indians when there are no more of them living in the area?"

Roger leaned back, arranging his features into a semblance of careful thought. A consummate actor, he presented exactly the image he desired.

"No. Can't say that I do," he lied smoothly. "I'd imagine it reverts to the public domain. That the county would list it for sale."

"It does become public land, right enough. Only it's federal."

Exactly why I can easily wind up owning it, Roger gloated silently. Bribing federal bureaucrats is considerably easier than dealing with the locals. The land in question means nothing to them and the money always looks good. Roger affected a fleeting smile and shook his head before he made reply.

"Well, then, there goes any reason for me being involved. Surely someone would research such a thing first. You know as well as I how hard it is to *get* anything from the federal government. Their idea is to *take*. So, the whole matter would be pointless."

Horton's scowl slipped into an expression of doubtful resignation. "Perhaps you're right. All the same, we've come to the conclusion that it would be in the best interests of everyone involved if you were to conduct your activities elsewhere. Preferably outside San Diego County."

"But, Alonzo, what of my investment in New Town Development Corporation?"

"We, uh, are prepared to, uh, refund fifty percent of that at this time, with the remainder in two equal payments over the next, uh, six months."

"With interest, of course?"

"I think, Mr. Styles," Sheriff Hunsaker injected, "that you might consider the offer as is, to be most generous. Were you to, ah, make matters difficult, it might be that further investigation into the allegations of mass murder would be necessary."

"That sounds remarkably like extortion. You have no proof. . . ."

"That's right," Horton interrupted. "We have nothing to tie you to these depredations. Yet, your manner of conducting your business and the, ah, quality of your associates leaves us a likely place to proceed, provided there is reason to pursue the investigation. I'm sure you understand."

"I'm being run out of town?"

"Oh, nothing so crude. You're being invited to depart with your integrity intact, along with a return of your investment. You have land of your own. You can sell it for profit, keep it, or do as you like. It would be nice, though, as the sheriff said, if you left San Diego County."

Roger spread his hands in a wide gesture, palms up. "What choice have I, gentlemen? How . . . soon does this have to be effected?"

"By the end of the week, I would say," Horton offered.

"Well, then, never fear. I'm certain something can be arranged by then. Now, good day, gentlemen. And don't slam the goddamned door on the way out."

Chapter 8

Ironically, the Butterfield way station at the top of the grade happened to be located in a valley nearly identical to and only a mile from the peaceful meadow where the avenging party of Indians had gathered prior to their attack on the stage. After the beleaguered coach rattled in, Issac Hughes became feverish, and he suffered waves of pain from his wound in courageous silence. A piece of the arrowhead had struck bone and broken off. The crude tools available on the coach had not been adequate to remove the flint point or the fragment.

"He'll need a doctor soon," Rebecca advised the station agent when Manuel and Lone Wolf eased the wounded driver down from the seat.

"I can see that, miss. Uh, I'm sorry. Didn't mean to snap at ya. Ike's a good friend. I'm upset about this, is all. Why'n hell, after more'n a hundred and fifty years would them Diegueños decide to take to the warpath?"

"I said the same thing, Waldo," Issac grunted as he was carried to the interior of the depot.

"Someone's stirrin' 'em up," Waldo Pieper suggested. "There's been some attacks on villages. I know that for a fact. Young Juan Lachusa usually works for me, as you know, Ike. Well, the last week or so he's been comin' late or not at all. He did tell me that a couple of their villages had been wiped out. Everyone killed."

"Any idea who is behind it?" Rebecca asked earnestly.

"Nobody I could name," Waldo allowed. "Juan said the ones who did it were definately *xaiqo*, white men."

"What did they look like? Any descriptions?"

Waldo snorted his amusement through his nose. "You know how it is with Indians, miss? To them, all us white folk look alike. Here," he went on, directing his attention to his injured friend. "Just ease him down over there. Lemme get a look at that wound."

Outside, Hester hovered close to Manuel Osuna while he supervised the change of teams. Hands behind her like a little girl wanting a favor, she twisted from side to side and batted her eyes to make them shine brightly. At first, Manuel ignored her, intent on his task. Once it was accomplished, he turned and smiled.

"We sure had a close one back there," he allowed.

"You were so brave," Hester gushed. "Why, I don't think we could have survived if it hadn't been for you. May I call you Manuel?"

"Uh, sure. Your name's, uh, Hester?"

"That's right. Manuel, I don't know exactly how to say this. I, uh, I've never known anyone so young to be so brave before this. Why, you can't be much more than three years older than me."

"I've never thought of it that way. A fellow does what he has to. Uh, how old are you?"

"Seventeen."

Manuel brightened. "You're right. I'm exactly three years older." Manuel reached out and took Hester by an elbow. "We're gonna have to wait for a replacement driver. One of the men sleeping now. While we do, may

I show you around? This is a beautiful little valley."

"I'd like that ever so much, Manuel. Do you live close to here?"

"No. My home is to the north and west of here."

"What town is it?"

For a fleeting moment, Manuel felt embarrassed. "It isn't a town. It's a rancho. Los Vallecitos de San Marcos."

"Oh!" Hester cried brightly. "What a pretty-sounding name. What does it mean in English?"

"The Little Valleys of Saint Mark."

Hester pulled a face. "Oh, it . . . sounds important."

"It is, in a way, I suppose. The rancho was granted to my great-uncle on my mother's side, Don Jose Maria Alvarado, in eighteen-forty. It's, ah, my, er, inheritance from my mother."

"Oh, my, then, I suppose that makes you, ah, rather . . ."

"Wealthy? Yes. I imagine so."

"What of your father?"

"He is Julio Osuna, grantee of San Dieguito Rancho."

"You're . . . you're quite an important person, then. Why is it you work for the stage line?"

Manuel shrugged. "I'm not sure, really. Only . . . I'm not ready to settle down. Being a ranchero is serious business. Long, hard hours, cattle to tend, grapes to be harvested, crops to be sown, all the boring details of running a large agricultural enterprise."

Hester suppressed a giggle, though not entirely. "You talk so seriously about this. It's not like your usual self."

By then the pair had reached a small cluster of live oaks. The branches spread wide, inviting them to enter the pleasant circles of coolness. At Manuel's direction, they turned back and gazed across the meadow.

75

"Sometimes, Hester, I . . ." Manuel shrugged. "I don't know who I am. Or maybe who I want to be. There's the young, dashing *ranchero*, attending the balls, courting the lovely young ladies, going to Mexico City, or Salamanca or Madrid to continue his education. Then I see the freedom from decisions and hard, dull hours in an office, the chance to meet more people, learn about this new country we've become a part of. Oh, I know, Mexico lost California to the *yanquis* thirty years ago. Even so, it's all new to us down here in the south.

"California culture centered on Monterey, San Francisco, the Sacramento valley. That's where the big money is and that's where the *grin* . . . uh, Americans went. We're small, except in land area. Did you know that there were never any Spanish land grants in San Diego County? Not until after independence, when Pio Pico was governor, did parcels of land get granted for service to Mexico. So, we're not any great and ancient aristocracy hereabouts."

Manuel Osuna paused, gazing off over the valley, made more delightful by the close profile of Hester Claymore. A warmth kindled in his loins and spread outward through his compact, muscular body. Of a sudden, he strongly desired this beautiful *gringa*. He all but reached out and embraced her.

"Were there many . . . before you decided on this life, did you, ah, court a great many young women?"

Manuel chuckled. "Me? No, I'm afraid not. I have always been a bit shy when it came to women. Surprised?" he inquired when he saw her reaction.

"Uh, no. Er, yes. I mean, you're terribly handsome, you know. And I naturally thought, especially after you described your, ah, other life, that . . ."

"If my shyness would let me do what I desperately want to right now, you'd be in my arms and soundly

76

kissed," Manuel blurted.

"Then . . . why not be the dashing *ranchero* and overwhelm me with your delightful kisses?"

Both young people started at this bold statement, and then Manuel made a hesitant move to take her in his arms. Hester literally leaped into his embrace, her wrists crossed behind his neck, face upturned, eyes closed, awaiting the rapture of his lips. Only a slight bit awkwardly, Manuel responded with his mounting fervor.

When they parted, it was for but a moment. Manuel drew her to him and again kissed her with fire. Hester's lips parted, then her teeth, and she welcomed his probing tongue with a shudder of anticipation. One of Manuel's strong hands cupped a firm, budding breast. Hester sighed. She pressed against him and felt the proud protrusion of his erect maleness. She had been soiled, she believed, beyond redemption, as a captive in the Paiute village. As a result, she had determined at the time never to be sullied again by the touch of a man.

Now she found herself consumed with an unbearable longing as she tore frantically at Manuel's clothing. The pressure of his fingers on her breast became stronger. A soft moan escaped from Manuel's throat. Hester slid her hand inside the waistband of his trousers and sought out the tumescent organ that lay waiting there. With a force of will that resembled violence, Manuel broke off their lovemaking.

"No!" he cried. "Not now, not like this. I . . . I . . . oh, Hester, I can't deny that what I want most is to make love with you. Only here . . . somehow it seems . . ."

"It seems divine, to me. Could there be a cleaner, more beautiful, more peaceful place to join ourselves in the love we feel?"

77

Grinning, hating himself, Manuel bent down and kissed the hollow of her throat. "No. You're quite right about that."

Driven by their close brush with death, the two young people quickly removed their clothes. Hester sighed with delight at her first view of his long, slender manhood. Impulsively she reached out and grasped it firmly. Slowly, she stroked him. Manuel shuddered and brought trembling fingers to the upturned nodes of her nipples. Hester sighed. They kissed again. Gently, Manuel lowered her to the ground. He stood above her for a long moment, then he knelt.

"I'll be careful, beloved," he murmured.

"Yes, do, but, please, please hurry."

Slowly he entered her, going deeper, deeper. Hester trembled and silently pleaded for more. Manuel tingled with a sensation that no other woman had ever given him. Their bodies blended together, joined by the pulsing shaft that had pierced her to the depths. With agonizing leisure, Manuel began to thrust.

And the world whirled around them.

Rebecca Caldwell looked up from the soft folds of the blanket that shielded her naked shoulders from the rough ground. "Ian," she declared with a sigh. "I have a feeling that right about now, Hester is enjoying the very same happiness I am."

"What? How? Do you mean . . ."

"Calm down. She's a grown woman now. She can decide these things for herself. We've gotten rather close, you know. I sort of . . . sense a feeling of magnificent pleasure and release."

"My God! But, who?"

"Manuel Osuna, I presume. After what happened in the Paiute village, it's a good thing. She needs to realize that not all men are beasts. Osuna is a young gentleman. A grandee, as the Spanish-speaking people put it. Quite wealthy and well educated. In matters of love, as well, I imagine."

"Do you think he could ever be up to something like . . . this?"

Sharp, jolting shivers of ecstasy cascaded through Rebecca's body when Ian buried his face between her legs. She moaned and began to writhe when his tongue found the most sensitive spot and caressed it with wild abandon. Ian's bold organ swelled rapidly and painfully demanded attention. Carefully he maneuvered himself so that Rebecca could encounter it.

Her lips fluttered like butterfly wings around the engorged, ruby-red tip of his phallus. He trembled with delight and exerted even more energy on his gift of pleasure. Rebecca responded in kind. She sighed in abandon and sought to give and get the maximum. How wonderful Ian could be. How perfect their loving. As her hips began to gyrate faster she felt a gigantic crescendo approaching and wanted to savor the delicious feelings he was arousing.

He groaned in utter pleasure. On they strove, seeking to achieve perfection, eager to explode over the pinnacle into sensual oblivion. Rebecca seemed to burn with an inner, invisible flame. Her body grew slickly moist, her heart thudded in her chest, and she felt her senses reeling, driven off balance by unending sensation.

Oh, glorious, glorious, glorious! The shriek of completion came, though muffled by Ian's bulk. Then, without hesitation, he skillfully began to draw her upward for yet another waterfall of erotic play.

"Aaaaah!" Ayyyyyeeeee! I-I-I-Ian!" Rebecca wailed, whirling off through a galaxy of untrammeled joy.

Brown and sere, all life burned out by the relentless

sun of the summer just passed, the grass and brush of Rancho Jamul looked forbidding and unproductive to Roger Styles as he stood before the large adobe building that had once been the main ranch house. The stucco-plastered walls had broken away in places to reveal the rust-hued blocks of dried mud. All the same, he mused, those walls were three feet thick. The whole structure, built around a central courtyard, resembled a fortress. For that Roger gave thanks.

"This is it, Roger," Dooley Walsh declared with a touch of pride.

"That outer wall there," Roger responded, pointing behind them.

A low, rambling wall, some three feet high where it remained intact, described a boundary around the hacienda, some sixty feet from the building walls. It had decayed drastically with lack of attention and needed work to restore it.

"It can be built up as high as you want. All it takes is time and the men to do it."

"What about these squatters living on the place?"

"We can put 'em to work or run 'em off, whatever you prefer."

"Bring their leader to me, if they have one. If not, find a man who will act as a spokesman for the bunch of them."

"Yes, sir. Meanwhile you'd best be movin' in."

"Has the place been cleaned?"

Dooley shrugged. " 'Bout as good as the likes of our boys can do."

"Then you'd better arrange for some of those squatter women to come here and make it decent. Tell them all that if they want to stay here, they'll have to work for the, ah, *patrón*. Then bring their representatives back. Is there water?"

"Oh, yeah. Three wells, the creek, and some seep

springs behind the house in that narrow canyon."

"Excellent, Dooley. Now get along with it, so we can see some progress before evening."

After his chief henchman left on his errands, Roger strode around this easternmost portion of Rancho Jamul. Long abandoned, the property still showed considerable promise. The huge, two-story house needed little in the way of repair. He stalked through dusty rooms, peered into cabinets fastened to the inner walls, inspected the drafts on the beehive fireplaces in every chamber. The inner courtyard, or patio, had become a riot of vegetation. Left to go wild, it had become a mixture of living and dead plants, an algae-slimed fountain at the center.

As for the property itself, it couldn't be in a better location. Unseen from the main road, protected from the prying eyes of neighbors by high, granite-strewn hills, with ample water and a potential for growing enough crops and livestock to be self-sufficient, he couldn't ask for more. It would, he fervently believed, be the ideal location for the headquarters of the soon-to-be "Emperor of California."

"Soon now," he declared aloud to himself. "Soon, I shall have it all!"

Chapter 9

Half a dozen two-story buildings, including the Julian Hotel, dotted the skyline of the small mountain mining town. The raw dirt streets had been sanded and the main drag cobbled for a distance of three blocks in an attempt to give a touch of class to the community. A smelting works belched black, acrid smoke, and the clang of its stamp mill rang off the surrounding mountaintops. Crows and red-tail hawks wheeled in the air above. The coach, bearing Rebecca Caldwell and a blissful Hester Claymore, rattled into Julian, to create an instant sensation.

"Looka that," a towheaded, blue-eyed youngster said to his brown-skinned companion. "See them holes? Hey!" he yelled. "The stage has been shot at."

Adults picked up the call. By the time the Butterfield mudwagon stopped before the depot, a crowd of some thirty people had gathered.

"Where's Ike?" a man called out.

"What happened?"

"You'll not believe this," Manuel answered their insistent queries. "We were attacked by Indians."

"No! That can't be," a instant doubter stated flatly.

"Who were they?"

82

"Don't know for sure. Diegueños, I think," Manuel replied as he climbed down from the driver's box.

"Diegueños? Why, they've never caused anyone trouble," a man in the black dicky and Roman collar of a clergyman said.

"It wasn't angry rabbits that put those bullet holes in the coach," Manuel growled. "Ike took an arrow in his leg. He's laid up at the way station. We all had a bad time of it. *Por el gracia del Dios*, we survived."

"These ladies," a portly man in an expensive suit, though one wrinkled beyond recovery, demanded. "Were they aboard at the time?"

"Sure were," Manuel replied.

"Ladies, I'm Malcom Dobson, the *Julian Mercator*. I'd like a few words with you about this harrowing experience."

Rebecca coolly studied the newspaper man. He had food stains on his shirt front and cigar ashes on his vest and coat lapels. A glint of avarice lighted his small, narrow-set eyes, and his bulbous nose and red spider-webbed cheeks proclaimed him a drinking man. She developed an instant dislike for him.

"There isn't much to tell. The Indians attacked us and we fought them off."

"The, ah, men in your party, you mean," Dobson responded with a flat statement.

"No. Hester and I did our part."

"I have the headline now," Dobson said dreamily, ignoring her response. " 'Two Travelers and Stage Crew Fight Off Deadly Indian Attack. Save Lives of Imperiled Young Women.' How's that?"

"Apparently you didn't hear me clearly, Mr. Dobson. I said that Hester and I fought the Indians also."

"Oh, but that would never do for a news story," Dobson blustered. "What's needed is a stirring tale of heroism."

83

"Mr. Dobson, I personally killed two of the marauders. However, I'm not all too anxious for publicity. Still, if one is to write a news story, shouldn't it contain the truth?"

"Certainly, certainly, madam. Only it is the responsibility of the reporters and the editor to determine *which* truth is to be told."

Angered by this pompous man's smug condescension, Rebecca narrowed her eyes. "Then you intend to write this incident up the way you see it, rather than how it actually happened?"

"Of course. That's what freedom of the press is all about."

"Well then, when you have it completed, you can take that newspaper of yours, roll it up in a tight cylinder and shove it up your . . ."

"Becky!" Ian Claymore interrupted from beside the coach. "Gently, my dear, gently."

"Who might you be, sir?" Dobson inquired, on firmer ground addressing a member of his own sex.

"Ian Claymore. The Reverend Ian Claymore."

"Hummm. I . . . see. So then . . ." Dobson began, glancing to Lone Wolf. " 'Lone Male Passenger and Valiant Crew Save Stage from Disaster.' That ought to do it."

"That's another crock of shit," Lone Wolf growled.

"What? What's that?"

"I said you're full of road apples. Ian and I did our share, true enough. Rebecca and Miss Claymore also defended themselves. I'd suggest you spend more time learning the facts and less concocting lying headlines. Or you might have opportunity to do exactly what Rebecca suggested with that paper you put out."

Dobson's mouth worked like a hungry fish. His complexion took on a tentative beet hue and his breath came in rough snorts. At last he recovered the ability to

84

speak.

"You'd do well to not attack the sanctity of the press. Remember, the pen is mightier than the sword," he challenged darkly.

"Oh? Tell that to those Indians back on the road," Rebecca replied sweetly.

"Move back, folks," the depot agent called from the porch in front of the Butterfield station. "Make room for these people to come inside. There's a report's got to be made out."

After every last detail of the attack had been related, Rebecca, Lone Wolf, and the Claymores left the Butterfield terminal. To their relief, the crowd had dispersed, attracted to other events. Rebecca nodded toward the center of town.

"I'd like to stay over a few days. This attack has made me curious. What I'd like to do is . . ."

When she did not continue, Ian urged her on. "What is that?"

"Oh, nothing. They say the Julian Hotel has the best accommodations. Shall we take rooms there?"

"Come on, Rebecca," Lone Wolf prodded. "You might as well say it now. We'll find out before long, anyway."

"I think what I would like to do is pay a call on the Indians. Find out their side of the story."

"Have you lost your senses?" Ian demanded.

"Not in the least. They must have a reason for attacking whites. I suspect that the answer is whites have been raiding among their villages for some unknown reason. Whites employed by Roger Styles."

"Becky," Ian attempted reason. "You've become obsessed with this Roger Styles business. Can't there be some other reason?"

"There might be, but mine seems the most likely."

"How can you say that?"

85

Rebecca replied with an enigmatic smile. Wait until I get you alone, she seemed to be telling the sandy-haired young minister.

Dust rose from where ten men dug in the claylike soil. They loaded burlap pouches and carried these to where five *adoberos* mixed the earth with straw, crushed oyster shell, and water. The resultant material they poured into wooden forms and slapped them smooth. The work was going well on heightening the outer wall of his *estancia*, Roger Styles thought with pleasure. Likewise, the wives of these workmen, and twenty more, had done wonders for the abandoned main house of Rancho Jamul. Far enough removed from the lush, fertile valley where the new headquarters of the ranch had been established, not a soul had passed by or stopped to ask questions.

Today, though, proved an exception. Ten men, led by a squint-eyed ruffian in a black, tight-fitting outfit and a large wide-brimmed sombrero had arrived. Sunlight glinted off the bright brass cartridges in their crossed bandoliers. They waited politely outside the hacienda while the newly established *major domo* brought word to Roger.

"Some men to see you, *patrón*," the graybeard announced.

"Who are they?"

"I do not know, *señor*. They have the looks of *bandidos*," he added in a tone of distaste.

"Have their leader, if there is one, come in. Wouldn't it be amusing, Uvaldo, if they came demanding tribute?"

A ghost of a smile illuminated the old man's face. The seventy or so heavily armed men working for the *patrón* looked little more than bandits themselves. But it was not for Uvaldo to question. They were the *patrón*'s men, and that was enough. He shuffled out to the forecourt.

"The *patrón* will see your leader now. The rest remain. I shall have a woman bring you refreshment."

"*Gracias viejo*," the man in black thanked the old retainer. "How is your *patrón* called?"

"*Don* Rogelio, if it pleases you, *señor*."

"And if it doesn't please me, *viejo*?" the tall, lean bandit teased.

"*Mas ó meno*, it is not my problem. Come in, then. He awaits you."

Striding boldly along the cool inner passageway to the patio, Rudolfo Mateo exuded the air of a man of power and security. Gone were the rotted vegetation, the broken and wild plants. The fountain had been emptied and scoured. Sparkling clean water spurted from the outlets now, to make pleasant tinkling sounds when it struck the surface in the basin. The trees had been trimmed and all the inner-looking windows washed. A far cry from the last time Rudolfo had been by this way. Perhaps this Don Rogelio might turn out to be a weakling. Though that was not what he had been led to expect. Through a pair of french windows, Uvaldo led him to a tastefully appointed office.

A slightly pudgy *gringo* rose from a swivel chair that had been drawn up to the front of a rolltop desk. He wore fine clothing, though not so delicate as to be ridiculous in the rugged back country. A smile brightened his clean-shaven face and he extended a hand in welcome."

"*Buenas tardes, Señor, ah . . .*"

"Mateo. Rudolfo Mateo, Don Rogelio. *Con mucho gusto.*"

"*Y tusted equalmente, Don Rudolfo.*"

"I had not been told you spoke our language."

Roger produced a sheepish grin. "I do not. Only a

few words a day that I pick up from my campasinos and add to my vocabulary. Here, take a chair. What brings you to Casa Rogelio?"

Rudolfo accepted the offered seat. "It could be one of . . . several things," Rudolfo evaded.

"Such as what?"

"I might be here on behalf of my *jefe* to demand tribute."

Roger produced a scowl and a hooded-eyed glare. "I have sixty-five experienced guns to back me, Don Rudolfo."

Rudolfo shrugged and produced a small smile. "Or I could be here to offer the services of myself and my men."

"Now that sounds much more acceptable. Considering that Uvaldo informs me there are but ten of you. On what conditions would you be willing to join my band of *pistoleros*?"

"Ah-ha! A man of directness. I admire that. Though a blunt approach to business can sometimes cause certain, ah, problems, no?"

"*Aqui en Casa Rogelio no tienes pinche problemas*," Roger replied rapidly.

Rudolfo all but slapped Roger on the back. "You have an amazing grasp of our idiom, Don Rogelio. 'We don't have any little problems,' eh? Remarkable for a *gringo*. So then, to answer your question," he went on in a milder mood, "We ten might consider joining you, Don Rogelio. However, under the right conditions I can promise you the addition of another forty expert guns."

Roger whistled softly. "That would give me a veritable army. I'm impressed, Don Rudolfo. What would this largess cost me?"

"Our association would be in the form of a joint endeavor. We'd share equally. At least you and our *jefe* would divide the spoils that way. Each would then take care of his followers."

"Ummm. I have a great deal more mouths to feed and pockets to fill than your *jefe*. Perhaps a seventy-thirty split?"

"That's not what *el* . . . er, not what my *jefe* would find acceptable. Say . . . sixty-forty?"

"You do love to bargain. I would have to see your men, see them in action before I could decide."

"Of course. When would it be convenient?"

"We're making a little visit on a Diegueño village the day after tomorrow. In fact, part of my loyal contingent is making ready to ride out this afternoon. Until then, make yourselves at home. *Mí casa es su casa*. I'll have Uvaldo arrange everything."

Rudolfo rose, extending his hand. "*Muchas gracias*, Don Rogelio."

"I think I can promise this will be a mutually rewarding association."

Chapter 10

Screams died slowly to whimpers and moans as Mateo's men exercised their lust on the bodies of some Diegueño girls salvaged from the attack. Even Roger had deigned to avail himself of some convenient release. He had selected a feisty young thing. Left unfettered, she pounded and clawed at him as he thrust himself violently into her. With each rip her slashing nails put in his skin, his excitement grew to greater heights.

Roger quivered and moaned while he impaled his small victim. She writhed and howled, sought to gouge out his eyes. Deliciously aroused, Roger released his grip on her silken hips to smash a fist into her face. The act of violence alone caused him to reach the pinnacle of release.

Then he shot her under the chin.

"*El es asqueroso*, disgusting," Rudolfo whispered to one of his men. "A swine. *Uno perverso*."

"Why don't we simply kill him and take over everything for ourselves?"

"That is for *el Coronel* to decide. Until then, we follow orders and tolerate that . . . *cabrón*."

Crackling flames announced the burning of the

village. The men completed their recreation and returned to horseback. Rudolfo Mateo rode beside Roger Styles. After a mile or so, he broached a subject of considerable interest.

"I know of a way to increase the profits so we have even more to share."

"How is that, Don Rudolfo?" Roger felt drained and happily sated.

"We take the boys and young men to sell to the mine owners in central Baja California. The girls of eleven to sixteen we sell to the whorehouses, the *putarias* in Mexicali. That brings a lot more than scalps."

"I'd considered something like that, only . . . what if any of them escaped to identify us later on?"

"Your men would not need to be a part of that. Leave it to us. All the same, we would share. Would that make my *jefe*'s proposal more attractive?"

"It certainly would. Indeed it would."

"For the next raid, then, eh? Tell the men not to kill those we can sell."

"Agreed."

Lighthearted, the vicious band of killers rode off into the early morning mist that clung to the peaceful mountains.

New stories of horror had replaced the stage attack as the prime topics in Julian. A postal rider came up from San Diego and excitedly related to the town idlers of coming upon a small cabin, burned to the ground, its occupants, the Miller family, all dead and lying in the yard. Fred Miller, his wife, June, and three children. Anger grew against the Diegueños. Dobson's newspaper ranted and raved, demanding retaliation. Rebecca's determination to visit the Indians grew. After a late breakfast, she and Ian walked through the center of Julian, heatedly discussing the matter.

"You're not going on some very likely suicidal quest to visit obviously hostile Indians, Becky," Ian commanded.

"Ian, I *must* go. I have no intention of going alone. Lone Wolf will come along. We did much the same thing with the Paiutes and got away with it."

"Only barely, let me remind you."

"The situation here is nowhere near that serious, so far."

"How can you be sure of that?"

"The Paiutes were in an all-out war, goaded by agents of Roger Styles. Here we have some people who have been attacked in their peaceful villages, people, I might add, who are not considered to be up to the skills and demands of warfare. They may have already done all they intend to do. No matter, I'm going."

"Becky, be reasonable . . ." Ian pleaded, abandoning his firm stance.

"There's one of those damned beggers now!" The familiar, unpleasant voice of Malcom Dobson bellowed from down the street.

Rebecca and Ian looked to where a small crowd began to gather. A slender, dark-complexioned young man seemed the center of a hastily formed circle of citizens. Still pointing the way, Malcom Dobson rushed toward the subject of his call of alarm.

"Filthy, murdering savage!" he shouted. "Defiler of women and children!"

"No doubt new headlines for his yellow sheet," Rebecca quipped as they, too, strode rapidly toward the crowd.

"You have a nerve coming in here after what your people are doing," the newspaper editor challenged as he arrived.

"B-but . . . Mr. Dobson," the youthful Diegueño sputtered, "You know me. Juan Lachusa. I'm not a murderer or a . . . whatever that other is. I come to Julian all the time. I work for the stage company."

"All the better to know the schedule and aid in the ambush three days ago."

"I . . . I heard about that. What I came for, though, I came to find the deputy. A whole village of my people was wiped out early this morning. Massacred. We need the law to help us."

"Good enough for them, I say," Dobson snapped. "Good enough for you, too, you blood-lusting savage. Sneakin' around here to plan an attack on Julian, weren't you?"

"No, I . . ."

"One of you get a rope. We'll string up this spying redskin!" Dobson shouted.

"Now I don't think that would be all that good an idea, Mr. Dobson," Rebecca Caldwell said coldly.

Dobson winced at the painful jab that accompanied Rebecca's placing the muzzle of her .38 Baby Russian revolver against his back, over one well-padded kidney. She held it firmly, steadily in place, and the newspaper editor's keen ears clearly heard the ratcheting of the hammer when she cocked it.

"Why don't you listen to what he has to say?" she suggested in a low voice. "Or would you rather have me blow your kidney out the front of your stomach?"

Dobson made a sick, gagging sound and his liver-spotted skin turned a pallid, greenish white. He darted his glance back and forth at the people around Juan Lachusa, then craned his neck in an attempt to look at Rebecca.

"Don't move around so violently, Mr. Dobson. It might cause my trigger finger to twitch. You wouldn't want that, would you? Now tell these people to let him go before I blast you in half, you son of a bitch."

"Uh, er, uh . . . l-let him go, folks. We'll have

Deputy Spears get the truth out of him," Dobson bleated.

"Ian, would you please go find the resident deputy?"

"Of course, my dear. Right away."

When the crowd stepped away from Juan Lachusa, a seething Malcom Dobson turned on Rebecca Caldwell. "This'll be all over the front page. I'll have you charged with assault, with attempted murder. You'll pay for this."

"What about your trying to incite violence, form a lynch mob? There are ample witnesses to what you did. I'm sure this young man, and the Reverend Claymore, will be willing to swear that's what you were doing."

A grinning Juan Lachusa stepped to Rebecca's side. "I sure owe you for that, ma'am. Thank you. And I'd be proud to tell the deputy exactly what Mr. Dobson said and did. I'm Juan Lachusa. And a village did get destroyed this morning."

"Tell the deputy all about it. In the meanwhile, I'm Rebecca Caldwell. I would like to know what is happening in these mountains. Our stage was attacked by Indians three days ago, and there have been stories about the raids on your villages as far away as Yuma. What I want to do is come talk with your elders, to the chiefs' council, if there is one."

"You look a little like one of us."

"I am," Rebecca told him. "I'm half-Sioux."

"Then maybe they would listen to you and stop the terrible things that are happening. When I return to Baron Long, I'll tell the chiefs."

"Thank you. Say that I will be leaving for there within two days. And, uh, how do I get there?"

Juan quickly gave her directions to find the reservation. He finished only a second before Ian returned. Rebecca had long since returned her purse gun to its place of concealment, so she presented a pretty, stylish image to the lawman who accompanied the minister.

"What's going on here?" Deputy Lon Spears demanded.

"Deputy, another of our villages has been raided. Everyone killed. Can't you come and look it over, do something about it?" Juan Lachusa pleaded forcefully.

"Not in my jurisdiction. I'm sorry, Juan. Sheriff Hunsacker feels the same way—we want to help, believe it should be our job to do so. Only the big-shot government in Washington don't ever get around to doing anything about it. Where was this? For the record, anyway."

"Down by Potrero. Maybe twenty-five people. All killed and scalped."

Spears scowled. "That's an awful thing, Juan. I'll do what I can, which is make a report from what you tell me and send it to the sheriff. Maybe we can get this thing settled so we can do something about it."

"It would be a good idea, deputy," Rebecca said quietly.

Dressed in the comfortable traveling garb of an Oglala woman, Rebecca Caldwell slid a moccasin-clad foot into the stirrup of her saddle. She swung up with ease and looked over confidently to Lone Wolf.

"We should make it there by noon tomorrow. It's fortunate Juan Lachusa can accompany us."

"We'd be crazy to go without him, you mean."

"Please. Don't you start in on me. What we're doing is right. And we're ready for any contingency."

Rebecca patted the thick leather of the saddle gun holsters that held her brace of Smith Americans. The long-barreled six-guns sat close at hand, draped over the pommel of her saddle. Below, to her right, the walnut stock of a model '73 Winchester protruded from its scabbard. Lone Wolf, she knew, had outfitted himself equally well. She swung the nose of her Appaloosa, Śila, to the right and walked him slowly down the main street of Julian. They would meet Juan at the sheriff's small office.

Both Ian and Lone Wolf had prevailed upon her not to leave for the apparently hostile camp until Juan could complete his business with the lawmen and act as a safe conduct guide. Impatient to be doing something, anything, Rebecca had nearly gone off alone. All the same, they would now travel together. Ian would remain behind with his sister, to make arrangements to go on into San Diego. A block away from the Julian Hotel, Juan waved a greeting to them.

"All ready, I see. One pack horse should do it."

"We hadn't considered taking even that," Rebecca told the young Diegueño.

"It gets cold at night in these mountains, as you know. And what about cooking meals?"

"Juan, Lone Wolf spent ten years with the Crow. I lived with the Sioux for five years. We know how to make do over an open fire." When she saw the youth's hurt expression she hastened to make amends. "I didn't mean that as a criticism, Juan. I only wanted to point out that we aren't spoiled, uh, *xaiqo* who need pampering on the trail."

Her warm, sweet smile erased all of Juan's misgivings. "Let's ride then," he said brightly.

They made good time through most of the day. The trail led down through the gentle notches on the west slopes of the Cuyamacas. Grass and sagebrush dotted large meadows, along with the sturdy native manzanita. Here and there blue-green clumps of yucca and agave thrust spiked leaves toward the sun. In late afternoon, clouds began to roll in from the west.

With them came a brisk, chill wind that lashed the

branches of oak and pine. The sky darkened, fat, black bellies of thunder clouds replacing the seamless blue above their heads. Juan studied the weather with growing concern.

"We could be in for a bad one," he remarked when the last bit of horizon disappeared into swirling gray.

"What are the storms like up here?" Rebecca inquired.

"Two kinds, usually. Either slow, misty rain with a low, chill wind, or some of the most violent, noisy downpours you could imagine. Even when it snows, the wind blows ferociously."

"Not what I'd like to encounter."

Juan snorted in amusement. "Long ago, my people used to go hide in caves when the winter storms came. Or journey down to the desert until better weather. Now they shake their fists and curse the thunder god in Spanish."

"I think going to the desert makes more sense," Rebecca offered.

With a sound like a gigantic, growing wave breaking on a rocky shore, the wind suddenly gusted powerfully enough to move them in their saddles. Rebecca caught at her breath and watched swirling flurries of dark oak leaves form light brown funnels in the air. Tree limbs lashed and twisted in torment. All of the birds had fled from the sky.

"I thought that was one of your rainstorms," the White Squaw remarked.

"It can't be far behind. We'd better find shelter."

"Where?"

"Over there. That's what the Mexicans named Luan Peak. There's a good-sized cave we can use. We'll have to hurry though."

Another violent burst of wind drove at them from the southwest. Juan had just started to speak again when lightning ruptured the sky. Its bright flash sizzled over them and erupted in the upper branches of a stately pine. Seventy feet above the ground, flames came into being and began to crackle voraciously at the resinous evergreen. The thunder pressed against the trio's eardrums with the force of a hundred sticks of dynamite. The horses trembled and rolled their eyes, showing mostly white.

"Now!" Juan cried out. "We have to run for it."

It took little urging to get their mounts to bolt into a gallop. Like the rustle of a million rats' feet, the hissing, seething rain raced toward them, their backs now turned to the tumult. Another dazzling bolt crashed into a slender pine and brought it down in a tangle of shattered limbs. Sila shied and tried to change direction. Rebecca fought the reins and wished for a simple Oglala hackamore. The air became cloying, heavy with ozone.

"To the right," Juan shouted over the cacophony of the storm. "Turn to the right."

Ahead, Rebecca could now make out an irregular spot of blackness in the gray face of the peak. Rain slashed at them and obscured their vision. With each pounding stride, the horses bore them closer. When the wind whipped the huge drops sideways, Rebecca could define the dark spot as a cave entrance. Fifty yards and they would make it. A ball of brightness bounded past.

Unlike anything she had experienced before, the crackling sphere hurtled across the ground, followed by another and yet a third. Hail began to slash at her exposed skin and thud painfully against her shoulders. Twenty yards and they would be out of the storm. A loud rumble and clatter warned of a rock slide as the suddenly saturated soil gave way on the slope to their left.

Juan disappeared into the cave as Rebecca desperately guided Śila around the tumult of slithering stones and mud. An instant later she sprang free and rushed for the shelter. Lone Wolf came close behind. Rebecca bent low and reined in as blackness enveloped her. The roar of the storm abated.

Soaked and chilled, she trembled as she dismounted and turned to look out at the deluge that had turned the world into a gray curtain.

"We'll be here for a while," Juan Lachusa said from beside her.

"At least we're alive."

"For the time being," Lone Wolf added as he entered the refuge.

Chapter 11

Outside, the elements continued to war against the mountains. Those inside the confines of the cave had no desire to venture onto the field of combat. At this altitude, many of the clouds sailed serenely up from the lower notches to collide directly into the boulder-strewn sides of the higher peaks. Ozone still tainted the air and the moisture deadened most odors. Intermittantly, thunder reverberated from the surrounding hills. Bright flashes of lightning strobed their movements. From further inside, Rebecca heard the scratch of a lucifer being struck.

Pale yellow light flickered a moment, then grew brighter as a torch of pine needles and twigs burst into life. Juan came forward. His earlier worry had been replaced by an expression of prideful glee.

"Now we have light to see by. There's wood stored back there. We can build a fire to cook our food. There is even a seep spring to water our horses."

"All the comforts of home," Rebecca said in a flat tone.

"The ground will be too wet to move until tomorrow."

"Then we might as well enjoy what we have," Rebecca concluded. She shivered. "I could use that fire right now. We're all soaked to the skin."

Soon a cheery blaze crackled against a blackened rock that gave evidence of frequent use in the past. Rebecca wanted to remove her dress, but refrained out of consideration for Juan. Then she snorted in self-derision. The men had peeled off most of their clothing to dry, why not she? After all, Juan was an Indian. Nudity probably meant nothing to him. She rose and pulled off her dress.

Immediately she felt better for it. Warmer, definitely. Lone Wolf and Juan seemed to take no notice of it. A few minutes later, Juan slid out of his trousers and hung them on a pole rack to dry. He was a well-formed young man, Rebecca noticed with pleasure. More accurately, a boy, yet well into maturing. His skin was smooth, unscarred, and glowing with health. He was quite well endowed, she noticed with a stirring flush that rose from her loins. Better not to think along that line, she chided herself.

"You might as well join the party," Rebecca told Lone Wolf.

Grinning sheepishly, the white warrior rose and pealed off his sopping leggings and loincloth. It had been a long time since Rebecca had seen Lone Wolf unclothed. The occasion had been identical to their present situation. They had never been lovers, though each had expressed a natural attraction for the other. Not that Lone Wolf had any defect. He had foresworn women because of his pursuit of a Crow medicine quest that demanded celibacy for its practitioners. A dratted inconvenience, he soon discovered, once he was back among his own kind. But one he followed religiously in order to reap the eventual reward. So, three naked people sat now, so close around the fire their shoulders touched, with only two of them feeling any stirring of desire.

Rebecca soon discovered undeniable evidence of this in Juan's rigid erection. He eyed her shyly, producing nervous, fleeting smiles and quick glances away. His breathing became a bit ragged. So did hers, she realized, awakening to the need that cried out within her. Not here, not now, she scolded herself. Not with this stripling young man who must be at least two years younger than herself.

There had been the twins, her sensual side reminded her. They had been only sixteen. And Bobby Rhodes, who had barely turned fifteen. What harm would it do, when they so obviously desired each other? Steam rose from their clothing as it dried rapidly. Rebecca tried to concentrate on that, instead of the pounding of her heart.

"There's more to the cave," Juan declared in a cracking voice. "It's an old dwelling place of our people. Would you like to see it?"

"Yes," Rebecca answered, a bit too rapidly. Forcefully, she got a grip on her runaway emotions. "Under better circumstances that would be interesting."

Juan cleared his throat before speaking. "That's true enough. At least we ought to wait until our clothes are dry."

"Yes," Rebecca answered again, absently, her mind on the likely implications of cave-exploring with this muscular young man.

"We should make it to Baron Long by a little after noontime tomorrow, provided there aren't any washouts that cause us to detour," Juan supplied, changing the subject.

"The sooner we get there the sooner we can find out about these raids," Rebecca agreed.

In half an hour's time they were able to redress. The usual conventions seemed to return with the clothing. At least there was no longer such a glaring physical display of amorous hunger. Rebecca's loins ached, though, for that satisfaction that right then only Juan could give her.

"We'd better fix something to eat," Lone Wolf suggested.

"Couldn't come too soon," Rebecca replied with forced cheerfulness. "I'm starved." She needn't elaborate for Lone Wolf's benefit on the nature of her hunger.

During the meal, the storm abated with the same suddenness of its beginning. Tension eased for all three occupants of the cave. From beyond the circle of firelight, the horses muttered in relief and eased their earlier, restive movements.

"Thank goodness for that," Rebecca breathed out. "I think we'd better get to sleep so we can leave at the earliest possible moment tomorrow."

"Good idea," Lone Wolf agreed.

Unfulfilled, Rebecca Caldwell rolled into her blankets, still aching for the adventure of sampling Juan Lachusa's rich endowments.

A long, grassy valley opened out from the narrow confines of the pass. Ancient oaks dotted the peaceful landscape and shaded the wooden and adobe houses sprinkled over the land. Near the center of the wide, bowl-shaped valley, Rebecca observed a large cleared space. Circling the bare ground she saw a number of *palapas* formed from tall, slender poles, the upper ends Vee-notched to hold the crosspieces. Over these a roof of brush had been woven. When they had ridden closer, she made out tables and a huge, rock-lined fire pit to the closer, northern side. Another fire ring of large stones had been placed at the eastern side. She didn't need Juan's explanation to realize what it was.

"The council meets there," Juan announced, pointing at the cleared ground. "And we have social dances, weddings, that sort of thing. Most of the time the children play there."

A great stir went up when Juan's identity became known. Boys of eleven or twelve ran out to greet him, only to stop short and stare in wonder at his companions. Several covered their mouths to stifle giggles and two lads hefted fist-sized stones.

"*Karap, Expa uru!*" one piping-voiced lad called out, pointing at Lone Wolf.

"*Umau!*" Juan barked at them. "You will not hit him, Bald Eagle."

"Are they your captives, Juan Lachusa?" an older boy inquired.

"No. They are my friends. They saved my life when some *xaiqo* would have hung me with a rope."

"Come to the council ground," a youthful warrior commanded as he trotted up. "Bring these strangers with you, Juan Lachusa."

With the youngsters jogging at their sides, the trio followed their escort to the council ground. More of the people of Barona gathered around, among them the warriors who followed Victor Occatillo. These latter scowled darkly and made threatening gestures. Rebecca tensed slightly and let her left hand drop closer to the butt of a Smith American.

She eased at sight of a procession of elderly men, most clothed like Juan Lachusa in floppy cotton trousers of an off-white color, roomy pullover shirts, and straw sombreros. In addition, most had blankets draped over their shoulders. With them came younger, stronger men, obviously war chiefs.

"Who are these white people?" a hard-faced man demanded in a language sharply different from Diegueño.

"They are friends, Victor Occatillo," Juan answered

104

in his own tongue.

"We have no *hiiqo* friends," the war leader spat.

"That's not so," Juan countered.

Carefully he explained the scene of his reception in Julian and the part played by Rebecca Caldwell in saving him from a lynching. Throughout, grunts of anger and surprise came from the listeners. When the recitation ended, the elders murmured agreeably and gave uniformly toothless smiles to Rebecca.

"What do they want here?" The harsh question came from Victor Occatillo.

"To learn what's been happening to our villages. Rebecca Caldwell, who is an Oglala women, believes she knows who's responsible for the attacks."

A tall, broad-chested man spoke out in a tone of authority. "She will speak to the council. Let the advisors gather. We'll meet after you have eaten and refreshed yourselves."

"Kill them now, I say," Victor Occatillo growled in accented English for the benefit of the hated whites.

The council members ignored his outburst and led the way to the west side of the circle, where the women of the village labored to prepare a meal. Venison roasted on an open fire. Nearby, women packed small birds, still with their feathers on, in clay and buried them in a deep bed of coals to bake. From a flat iron sheet a rich, corn aroma rose as a trio of older girls patted out flat cakes and put them on to cook. A small copper kettle, filled with bubbling grease of some sort, gave off a tantalizing, sweet nutty odor as the grandmothers rolled balls of acorn dough and dropped them in to make *chawee*. Inhaling the fragrant medley, Rebecca realized how hungry she had become.

"It all smells so good," she remarked with enthusiasm.

"It tastes good, too," Juan assured her.

"Do you have any idea as to how the council will decide?"

"Not really, Rebecca. Most of our people don't want war. Victor Occatillo came to us from the Cahuilla, along with twenty-four warriors. They're after revenge. Some of our young men have sided with him." Juan's tone changed, his face twisted with strong emotion.

"Victor and Two Dogs from here at Baron Long tried to attack a stagecoach. Several men were killed. The rest ran off. Those who came back said that even the women fought."

"I know," Rebecca replied gently. "Lone Wolf and I were with that stage."

Stunned, Juan could only stare at her for a moment. "Yet you come to help us? Why?"

"Because I believe I know who's responsible for all this killing. You work for Butterfield. You know that not all white men are evil. I only wish we had some better idea of how this would go."

"You can trust Ewi. He's head of the council now. He doesn't want war, but he's an old man. Cloud Belly went over to Victor Occatillo, as did Two Dogs. Many younger men still listen to them. Two Dogs used to be a friend of mine. At least before this talk of war. Him you might sway. Tomas Lujan, who's chief here at Baron Long, will side with Ewi. The chiefs from Rincon and Mesa Verde I don't know well enough to be sure of."

"Rather a mixed stew, then?"

Juan grinned. "That's a good way of putting it."

"Maybe I have just the stick to stir it with," Rebecca responded musingly.

When the council met, it took several minutes of heated discussion and a major bending of protocol to allow an outsider, and a woman at that, to speak before the assemblage. At last Rebecca received an introduction from Juan Lachusa, who would translate for her. Mustering her thoughts, she gave a thorough and concise presentation of her theory. After laying a background on Roger Styles and his apparent journey to San Diego, she came to the main point.

"Not long after Roger would have arrived in San Diego, your troubles began. He has a history of this sort of thing. He's evil, granted, but he's a man, like any other. He can be hurt, he can be destroyed. I'm here to plead with you to stop attacks on peaceful ranchers, miners, and the white people of the small towns here in the mountains. They are not responsible."

"What would you have us do?" Victor Occatillo scoffed. "Lie down and let ourselves be killed?"

"Nothing of the sort," Rebecca replied with strained diplomacy. "Lone Wolf and I are willing to help. We can go to San Diego, look around, and learn things in places where you can't so easily go. Once we find Roger Styles and his center of operations, we can lead you there. You can take the fight to the ones responsible."

There came several grunts of approval. Heads nodded in ascent and a murmur of whispered conversation rose in the circle of men. Victor Occatillo rose, his face one vast scowl.

"A *woman* talks to us about war? Have we lost our *cojones* that we must take council from a female? We'll kill all the whites or run them out and then there'll be no more trouble. That's the way to fight our enemies!"

"Victor Occatillo is right," Cloud Belly shouted, not bothering to stand. "Where there is one bad *xaiqu*, there will be more, and even more. We fight for more than revenge. We fight for our way of life, for freedom."

Ewi raised his eagle-wing fan to gain attention. "It is better to fight the real enemy than to waste our lives in a war we can't win. The *xaiqo* are too many. They have

107

many guns. We've little to gain by facing them with bows and war clubs."

"We can get guns!" Victor Occatillo interrupted. "A bow can get a rifle. One rifle can get us ten more. Ten can provide us a hundred. Can't you understand?"

Words seemed inadequate to the rage that boiled in the Cahuilla war chief. He turned about to rally his support. Some among the council turned their eyes away. Cloud Belly, Two Dogs, and a few younger hotheads stood to show their support. A thin smile of triumph spread Victor's lips.

"Hold!" Old Rattlesnake exclaimed.

His eyes burned with a fire known more often in youth. Slowly he rose and swept his eagle-wing fan over the gathered councilmen. Victor's smile slipped slightly. Even he must give some deference to age, so he seated himself once more.

"How are we to know if what they say is true?" Ewi asked Rebecca.

"We can go among the whites, dressed as they are. We can see and hear what we need to know. Messages can be sent to this council. If we are right, and I'm certain we are, you will know in time to prepare for one final, decisive battle."

"Your words are good," Ewi allowed. "We must discuss this and decide. Leave us and take your ease for a while. We'll summon you when we've agreed upon what to do."

Rebecca made a slight bow and turned away from the council circle. She and Lone Wolf retired to one of the brush-roofed pavilions across the clearing from the council fire. Tension grew to the point where even small talk was out of the question. Still no summons came. Half an hour passed.

"This Victor sounds too angry to make much of an impression," Lone Wolf offered.

"He's from another tribe entirely," Rebecca added hopefully. "Yet Cloud Belly is on his side and has a lot more influence. I'm worried."

"So am I."

"We can't afford to fail."

"Here comes Juan," Lone Wolf declared.

The tension could be cut with a dull axe.

"You're to return," the young Diegueño said curtly.

At the council ring, Rebecca and Lone Wolf stood before Ewi. He gestured to include the members, then pointed the tip of his fan at Rebecca.

"We are decided. Some still call for total war. It's not good. Older, wiser heads prevailed. Here is our will. From the time you return to the whites, you'll have five days to learn if this Roger Styles is the one behind the attacks. If this is so, we'll meet again and determine what to do. Juan Lachusa and three of our warriors will accompany you to act as messengers."

Hardly all she'd hoped for, Rebecca considered glumly. Still, it gave them a chance. She lowered her head in a sign of acceptance. Then another aspect of the situation recalled itself.

"What about the raids against the whites living in the mountains?"

"There'll be no more attacks on whites. At least not until we learn if you succeed or fail."

"We'll do our best," Rebecca promised.

Chapter 12

Fully a dozen varieties of insects hummed and buzzed over the surface of the narrow, shallow stream. They darted around the men's heads and sped off to inspect other prospects. The water trickled musically over smoothed rocks and swirled in algae-edged eddies, produced by the constantly shifting decomposed granite that formed the creekbed. Thirty Diegueño and Cahuilla warriors waited for final instructions. First they had to listen to a bitter harangue.

"Who are we to follow the orders of a mere woman?" Victor Occatillo snarled. "Stop fighting when already our enemies cower in fear? The council of the Diegueños is made of old fools. Men, if they still are, who have lost their courage. We must not give the whites time to gather their strength. Through that saddle is a big house," he finally began with his plan.

"The *segundo* of Rancho Cuyamaca lives there with his wife and three children. We'll surround the house, move in close without being seen. Then we'll attack on my signal. Kill them all. Run off some of the cattle.

Burn the *casa* like the whites do to us. We'll show the council who's right and who's wrong."

"What of the warrior woman and those who travel with her? Might they not come this way?" asked Two Dogs.

Victor produced an evil, twisted smile. "If they do, they'll die like the rest. Now, we must take our places."

Four-year-old Jamie Walker played happily in a mud puddle beside a large oak tree in the yard of the two-story log and adobe house in which his family lived. He'd pulled off his shoes, because he knew his momma would skin him if he got them messy. Likewise his shirt, because the day was warm. The britches of his denim overalls were sopping wet and smeared with the red-brown substance, as was his bare chest. Jamie chortled with glee and bent forward to lift up a double handful. He kept one eye trained on his intended target, old Bully, the family dog.

Bully romped playfully a few feet away. Abruptly he stopped his pursuit of his shaggy tail and assumed a straddled, stiff-legged stance, the hair on his thick neck rising as he bared his long, white teeth. A low growl issued from deep in his throat.

"Bully! Hey, Bully, what'cha doin'? You see a rabbit?" Jamie called in a high, thin voice.

The growl turned to a furious bark and Bully bounded three steps forward. An arrow's moaning hiss sounded a moment before the bark turned into a yelp of pain. Jamie rose, wide-eyed, and turned toward the house. Barefoot, he ran with all the speed his stubby legs could produce.

"Momma! Poppa! There's Injuns. They shot Bully!"

An arrow thudded into the ground an inch behind his left heel. Jamie choked on his words, which came in a frightened tumble. He gasped for air and tried to go

111

faster. Another shaft whirred past his right ear. He began to sob in terror. From the corner of his eye he saw his father rushing from the barn. He'd be safe after all, Jamie exulted. Then a bright pain exploded low in his back and he looked down to see the stone tip of an arrowpoint protruding from his bare belly. Jamie shrieked pitifully as he stumbled and fell forward.

"Jamie!" Thad Walker shouted in anguish when he saw his son fall.

A split second later the hat jerked from his head. Thad Walker heard the shot and saw the puff of smoke almost at once. He clutched a long-barreled Greener ten-gauge in his left hand. Thad had taken to carrying it since word of unrest among the Indians first went around. Now he lifted it to his shoulder at the sight of bronze figures emerging from the trees. He waited a heartbeat, then squeezed the trigger. A load of buck-shot spat from the righthand muzzle and sped toward the killers of his youngest child.

Two warriors cried out and stumbled, their flesh penetrated by burning double-aught pellets. A third made no sound at all, his chest pulped by the main part of the shot column. He whipped to one side and flopped on the ground, heels drumming. Thad saw his eight-year-old daughter, Prudence, run in the back door and heard the slam of the heavy bolt. To his right, more hostiles raced toward the front of the house.

"No!" he cried when Christopher, his thirteen-year-old, charged them on the buggy horse. "No, Chris!" he cried again.

Something shiny flashed in Christopher's right hand and descended in a swift arc. Thad blinked in disbelief when the weeding sickle his son wielded decapitated one of the howling warriors. Quickly the boy slid from the back of the trotting horse and he sprinted through the door.

"Hurry, Daddy!" Chris yelled.

Thad emptied the second barrel, reloaded and ran toward the house. He fired twice more and dropped three warriors. From inside, Chris opened up with a light squirrel rifle.

Victor Occatillo frowned. He hadn't counted on a dog. Not twenty yards away, the large, vicious-looking beast braced its legs and growled. Victor thought it would be easy. First the small boy playing in the mud, then the man at the barn. A young girl hung clothes on a line behind the house. She would die quickly, too. Then the woman and the other boy. He signaled Ignacio Arquero, a Cahuilla from his own band and the best shot with a bow.

Ignacio released a feathered shaft that buried in the dog's chest. Instantly the child jumped up and began to shout as he ran toward the house. *Mierda!* This could ruin the whole plan. Ignacio fired again . . . and missed. Ramon Hawk loosed an arrow. It, too, missed the slightly built little boy.

Ignacio's third projectile buried almost to the fletchings in the child's back. He stumbled and fell. Heeding the warning shout, the man came from the barn. Victor took aim with his Winchester. He fired and watched in frustration as the bullet spun the hat from his intended victim's head. Then everything seemed to go wrong.

In a group, the warriors rose from hiding and charged into the open. The man brought up his shotgun and fired. Two wounded and useless, one dead, Victor kept count. He could no longer see the girl, yet he knew she would by now have run to shelter in the house. Faster, Victor urged himself. From seemingly nowhere, the other man-child appeared, on horseback. He waved something bright and shiny in his hand.

Swiftly the towheaded youngster rode down on Ramon Hawk. A flash of light described an arc through the air. Ramon didn't even have a chance to scream. Numb with disbelief, Victor watched Ramon's head fly from his neck, followed by tall streamers of blood. The boy slid off the far side of his mount and ran to the front door. A moment later, the man fired his shotgun again.

Rebecca Caldwell reined in abruptly. "Did you hear that? Someone's doing some shooting over that way."

"Yeah," Lone Wolf agreed. "Don't sound like target practice."

"Not someone hunting, either," Juan Lachusa offered.

"It could be some of Roger's gang," Rebecca suggested.

"Not in that direction. Rancho Cuyamaca is over that ridge."

The trio exchanged startled glances. "They wouldn't have broken the agreement," Rebecca suggested.

"Not any of our people," Juan agreed. "I'm not so sure about Victor Occatillo. Maybe we'd better . . ."

"My thought exactly," Rebecca agreed.

Thad Walker made it through the thick front door and slid the heavy bar in place. Chris and his mother had already closed most of the shutters. Tears ran down Lila Walker's face, and her daughter sat on the fireplace hearth, curled in a ball, sobbing wildly.

"They murdered Jamie?" Lila's question came out sounding more like a statement.

"I . . . I'm sorry, dear. Yes, I'm afraid they did." Thad could think of nothing more to say.

"I got one of 'em," Chris said proudly. "Cut his head

114

off with a sickle."

Lila covered her face with her hands and began to sob. "Oh, son, son. How horrible."

"Might of been the one who got Jamie," the curly-haired boy offered matter-of-factly.

"The Lord says, 'Thou shalt not kill.' "

"Lila, if we don't do a heap of killin' right now, we're gonna wind up dead."

"Daddy's right, Momma. It's us or them. 'Sides, like Rever'n Talbot always says, 'the Lord helps them what helps themselves,' " Chris replied impudently.

"*Christopher!*" his mother admonished, stung by the words. "Do not blaspheme. Not this . . . this close to death."

"That's why we gotta fight, Mom." Chris poked the muzzle of his rifle out a firing loop and sighted on another warrior.

Lila bit at her lower lip. "I'll help you load. Prudence, dry your tears, dear. You come along and lend me a hand."

A bronze-skin-ringed eye appeared in one firing loop. Chris jabbed at it with a knitting needle he had snatched up from his mother's favorite chair.

Shrieking in agony, the Cahuilla warrior reeled away from the building, viscous fluid and blood streaming between the fingers he clasped over his right eye. A blast from Thad's Greener ended his agony.

Chris shouldered his rifle, the work of the needle completed, and fired again. His missed his target and handed the weapon to his sister, who passed it on to their mother. In exchange, Prudence handed Chris a heavier model '76 .45-60 Winchester. Although slightly built and small for his age, the wiry youngster easily absorbed the recoil as he worked the lever action and sent a rapid fire fusillade out into the yard, which broke the hostiles' initial charge.

"Go easy on ammunition, son," Thad advised.

"Yes, sir," Chris replied sheepishly. He'd only wanted to get even for Jamie. "Will they come back?"

"I don't know. Didn't even think these local bucks would ever put up a fight. Appears we were all wrong on that count. All we can do is wait 'em out and pray."

"What about . . . about Jamie?" Lila asked in a quavering voice.

"We'll have to let that go until it's safe," Thad told her regretfully.

"Over that way," Juan Lachusa directed. "The *segundo*'s house is just beyond that stand of oak."

"How many people there?" Rebecca asked.

"Hard to say. Some days only Walker and his family. Other times up to a dozen *vaqueros*."

"Let's hope there's plenty of them," Lone Wolf added.

"If they're the ones under attack, we won't have time to plan anything fancy," Rebecca declared. "We'll have to go in shooting and see what develops. How far to go?"

"Half a mile."

Panting from his hurried run, Cloud Belly came to where Victor Occatillo crouched in a jumble of rocks. The huge granite boulders provided excellent cover, except that it deprived the hostile Cahuilla of a field of fire. Cloud Belly pointed in the direction of the house.

"They are safe inside. Now what can we do?"

"Think for once, Ekwi-'etu. Use your head. Of what material is the house built?"

"Adobe and logs."

"What about the roof?"

Cloud Belly pondered a moment, then brightened. A wicked smile stretched his mouth into a grimace. Slightly cross-eyed, with a low, sloping brow, and a head wider at the back than the front, he resembled a rattlesnake preparing to strike. His tongue flicked out and wet his thick lips.

"It looks like bark," he offered.

"The whites call those *shingles*. But you are right. They are made of wood and will easily burn. It seems your men are better bow shots than mine. Take Ignacio along and have your braves fashion fire arrows. These they will shoot at the roof of the *casa*. Soon then the white devils will come rushing out to meet their deaths at our hands. It will be easy, as I have said from the first. Then we go to find more to kill."

Short, stocky, bronze-skinned Diegueño warriors appeared at the edge of the stand of oak. Each had nocked an odd-looking, fuzzy-ended arrow. They held three more in readiness in the hand that grasped their bows. Thad and Chris Walker watched uneasily while another of the group approached with a flaming brand.

He ignited the brush-tipped shafts and the warriors ran forward. They knelt as one and loosed their missiles. Before the first one had left the string, Thad realized the significance of their actions and poked his shotgun through the firing loop.

A scathing column of buckshot lashed out at the attackers. Two received painful wounds in their shoulders and chests. Chris took steady aim and hesitated only a fraction when the arrows fell short of the target.

"Closer!" a voice called in a tongue unintelligible to the whites. "You have to go closer."

The hostiles rose and moved in, albeit a bit hesitantly. When the one in charge ignited their missiles a second time, they fired, arching the trajectory of the shafts higher. Three of them smacked into the shingles above the heads of the beleaguered Walker family. Chris changed his point of aim and squeezed off.

A .45-60 slug smashed powerfully into Cloud Belly's shoulder. He dropped the burning flambeau and reeled backward, pain setting his teeth on edge. Determined to put the best face on everything, he allowed only a low moan to escape his lips. Chris levered in a fresh round and fired again.

Cloud Belly felt as though a horse had kicked him in the chest. Stunned, he plopped to the ground, in a sitting position. Slowly, dreamily, he looked down. A small, black hole showed above his right nipple. While he examined it unbelievingly, red fluid welled up and began to spill out.

"Moreno, take the brand and light more. . . ." he began to say, only to have speech taken from him by a gout of crimson that erupted up his throat and gushed from his mouth. A curtain of blackness descended over his eyes and Cloud Belly fell backward to strike the ground with his head. For a brief moment his heels pounded the hard-packed ranch yard, then he lay still.

"There's fire on the roof, Daddy," Chris said in a tight, worried tone.

"Not much we can do about it, son. By the way, good shooting."

"Thanks, Daddy. But . . . I can put it out. I'll take a rope and climb out through my bedroom window. Sis can send up buckets of water that way. Also my rifle."

"They'll kill you, Christopher," his mother protested.

"Not if Daddy keeps them away from the house long enough. Once I'm through I can shoot my way back to safety."

"Oh, I can't let you," Lila wailed. "I'd not live through losing both sons in the same day."

"It's the only way, Momma. That or we get burned up in here."

"The boy's right, Lila," Thad acknowledged reluctantly. A deep ache filled him at the thought of his only

118

other son dying.

"I've got to, Mom. It's the only way to save us."

Without waiting for a reply, Chris started for the stairs leading to the second floor.

Chapter 13

Sunlight cut golden shafts through the oak branches, threaded now with gray as the shingles on the Walker home blazed away. Victor Occatillo opened his eyes wide in surprise, and not a little admiration, when he saw the slight figure of the blond boy climb from a window and hoist himself up on the roof. The lad strung out a rope and began to haul up a rifle. Victor felt little threat. His men had ample cover among the trees. Then the youngster strained to lift a swaying wooden bucket. The Cahuilla war leader signaled his men to move in closer.

On the roof, Chris Walker heaved the container of water in a wide arc that doused three arrows with the first load. He lowered the bucket and picked up his rifle, eyes intent on the surrounding glen. Two hostiles appeared and drew back their bows. Chris fired.

A miss, though close enough to effect their aim. He chambered another round and squeezed off, searing a bloody line along the left shoulder of the nearer warrior. His sister yelled from the open window. Chris scrambled across the roof and drew up the rope with another three gallons of water. His activity provided an opportunity for Victor's men to move in closer.

They did so to their regret, as Thad Walker opened up with his shotgun.

Pellets slashed into two warriors, who had to crawl away on hands and knees. Victor scowled. Another bucketload and the boy would have the fires out. He needed to find a better means of attack. Brightening, he savored an idea that came clearly to him.

Large boulders on the far side of the house would provide close-in cover for more fire arrows to be used. The youngster couldn't protect both sides of the roof at once. Quickly Victor issued his orders.

"That's smoke," Rebecca yelled over the pounding of Sila's hoofs.

"From right over there," Lone Wolf acknowledged. "You can see the roof of the house."

"Someone's up there," Juan Lachusa remarked.

"Friend or foe?"

"Looks like Walker's older boy, Chris. Yes . . . he's putting out fires."

"We'd better hurry," Rebecca urged.

Weapons at the ready, they crashed through a stand of brush to the rear of a line of startled Cahuillas. The warriors attempted to reverse direction and fire at the unexpected relief force, only to die in a rattling hail of bullets. Rebecca's spotted-rump stallion ran down one hostile, whose wails cut off short under the sharp, pounding hoofs. Smoothly she fired to right and left, as did her companions. In a matter of seconds, the way lay clear to the house.

Rather than take this opening, they swung to the left and began to hunt down the attackers. Several bronze-skinned warriors fled before them, seeking to regroup with Victor and those who had gone to the back side of the house. Rebecca heard startled, pleased cries from inside the house. On the roof, a small boy waved at them, then crouched low at the peak and took aim beyond. It told her what she needed to know.

121

"They're regrouping on the far side. We ought to split up and go at them from two directions," she suggested.

"Not enough of us for that," Lone Wolf countered. "Play it safe."

The trio continued to press toward the barn. Two Diegueño warriors ran from its dubious protection in an attempt to join their comrades. Rebecca and Juan fired to wound, rather than kill. Rebecca's target flopped forward into the dusty ranch yard, both hands gripping a spurting wound in his right thigh. He'd need attention fast, the White Squaw made a mental note.

Juan's shot clipped the arm of a young man, who stumbled into the side of the corral and turned to face the surprise attack. He recognized Juan and threw aside his weapons, hands held in the air before him.

"Tie him up and take care of the other one," Rebecca ordered. "We're going after the rest."

Victor Occatillo crouched low in the cluster of boulders. His idea hadn't proved to be so good after all. From the roof of the house, the white boy sent round after round into the granite rocks. Showers of sharp-edged shards and bits of ricocheting bullets flew through the air. These cut skin and clothing and caused the war party to keep low, unable to effect any return fire. He looked up to see two mounted persons riding toward him. In a moment he recognized them as the woman, *Sinaskawin*, of the Oglala, and Lone Wolf, the white Crow warrior. While he watched, the woman holstered a big revolver and drew another one.

Fire and smoke spewed from the muzzle and a heavy .44 slug cracked into rock above Victor's head. Involuntarily he drew backward. Several of his men had already given up the battle and ran through the woods toward safety. He could not, he would not do that. With a roar of defiance, Victor stood upright and brought his rifle to his shoulder.

Before he could line up on a target, a force like the kick of a mule smashed into the butt-stock and showered his face with splinters. He dropped the useless weapon and clawed at his face to rid himself of the tiny points of distracting pain.

Lone Wolf recognized Victor Occatillo when he rose from the rocks. He realized the danger the blood-lusting Cahuilla represented for Rebecca and fired instinctively. His slug missed the intended target, Victor's head, though it destroyed the walnut butt-stock of the Winchester in the hostile's hands. He started to ear back the hammer once more when Rebecca shouted to him.

"Thanks, I owe you one."

She fired a shot that caused Victor to duck low and crawl away on his belly. All resistance had ended, yet Rebecca determined to locate the hothead and finish it completely. To do so, she had to dismount. Ground-reined, Sila waited with head down, though he twitched his hide at the odor of blood and gunsmoke. Rebecca started off through the rocks.

In moments she discovered blood spots. These she followed, cautious to avoid an expected ambush. The telltale red splotches became fewer in number. Not a wound, merely small cuts from rock chips, she surmised. Her prey would be most dangerous. Five long, tense minutes passed with no sign of Victor Occatillo. Then, without warning, Victor attacked her from behind.

With a howl of rage, Victor Occatillo leaped from a tall boulder that the White Squaw had passed only a moment before. At the last possible instant, Rebecca adroitly sidestepped, and Victor fell hard on the ground. Unfortunately, Rebecca had banged her head against a tree branch, which prevented her from following up her advantage. While pain-tipped stars whirled in Rebecca's head, Victor came to his knees.

A grunt of effort preceded his sudden launch forward, a knife in his left hand, stone-headed war club in his right. Rebecca ducked and raised her right arm to block the deadly swing of the knife. Their forearms met jarringly and the Smith American revolver fell from Rebecca's grasp. She jumped backward and pulled free her own slim skinning knife. A cruel smile creased Victor's face.

"That toy will do you no good," he smirked. "You are going to die."

"Not yet, Victor," Rebecca answered levelly.

She circled to her left, the knife in her left hand. While she did, her moccasined right foot kicked up a powdery substance made of decayed oak leaves and pulverized decomposed granite. It sprayed across Victor's chest and face. He blinked rapidly and pawed at his eyes with the back of his knife hand. Forced to retreat, he swung wildly with his war club.

Rebecca bit back a yelp of pain when the stone weapon smashed into the back of her left hand. Her knife flew into the underbrush. A fortuitous move for Victor. He saw his advantage through a haze of tears and bits of irritating vegetation. With a singleness of will he stamped his foot and bounded forward. To his surprise, his quarry didn't turn and run.

Rather, she stood her ground, her still capable right hand plunged into the small beaded pouch at her waist. Before Victor could take in the significance of this, Rebecca came out with the .38 Baby Russian in her hand.

The small revolver cracked loudly, then again. Twin

124

bullet holes, forming a figure eight, appeared three inches below and to the right of Victor's left nipple.

He staggered backward, eyes blinking rapidly. Words tried to form. A great lethargy seized him, and he began to sag. At last he forced sound from crimson-smeared lips.

"You've . . . you've finished me. It . . . it's n-not poss — ible."

Without a reply from Rebecca Caldwell, Victor Occatillo's eyes rolled upward, he sighed mightily, and fell to one side, relaxed into the terrible night of eternity.

Out of gratitude, the Walker family wanted to feast their rescuers. Rebecca and Lone Wolf declined, accepted final thanks from the relieved parents, and departed with Juan Lachusa. Birds had begun to sing again, and small, puffy clouds accented the cobalt sky. Slowly, Rebecca Caldwell shook off the eerie mood brought on by her fight with Victor Occatillo. By the time they reached Julian, an hour before sundown, she had resumed her usual good spirits.

"I could eat the biggest steak in town," she informed her companions.

"Let's see if we can find it for you, then," Lone Wolf replied.

"I'm for a bath first," Rebecca protested.

"Me, too," Juan Lachusa added eagerly.

"In the same tub?" Rebecca teased.

Juan blinked, then grinned engagingly. "If you insist."

"*Juan!*" Rebecca cried in flustered embarrassment.

Ian Claymore met the returning riders at the tie-rail of the Julian Hotel. He smiled warmly and offered a hand while Rebecca dismounted.

"I see your journey was uneventful," he began lightly.

"*Un*eventful! Let me tell you a thing or two, Ian Claymore. . . ." Rebecca began.

"Over dinner, please. I've good news about transportation into San Diego. We can leave by ten in the morning."

Cleaned of powder smoke and trail dust, Rebecca Caldwell and her companions joined Ian and Hester Claymore at the dining room of the hotel. They ordered from a menu featuring fresh oysters, lobster, duck, and roast venison. Elaborate napery and silver service graced the table. The community's elite, somewhat overdressed for the locale, filled chairs around the spacious salon.

"Now you can tell us what happened," Ian urged after ordering sherry for the ladies and bourbon for the men.

"I got an agreement from the tribal council to stop any indiscriminate attacks on whites," Rebecca told him excitedly.

"Only Victor Occatillo refused to honor it," Juan Lachusa added.

"Who's this Victor Occatillo?"

"A Cahuilla Indian from the desert, Ian," Rebecca informed him.

"What did that bring about?"

"He attacked the, ah, foreman's house at Rancho Cuyamaca."

"Then . . . the truce is over?"

"No. It stands as agreed."

"How'd you manage that, Becky?"

"Miss Rebecca killed Victor Occatillo," Juan informed Ian.

"Oh, my God."

Rebecca decided it politic, at least for the moment, to change the subject. "What about this trip to San Diego?"

126

"There's a special express coach that will go over by way of Campo and down through the southernmost pass to San Diego tomorrow. I've acquired tickets for all of us. Give the horses a rest."

Lone Wolf frowned, reflected by Rebecca for a moment before she spoke. "That'll be all right, I suppose. Better to leave them here at a good livery than to take our chances of having one as reliable there. Besides, the Indian trouble is up here in the mountains. We'll have to come back anyway."

During the several courses of the meal, Rebecca described the meeting at Baron Long, the agreement of the council, and the subsequent skirmish with Victor Occatillo's followers. After coffee, Lone Wolf and Juan excused themselves along with Hester, which left Ian and Rebecca alone.

"Hester's talking about preparing a picnic basket to take along."

"Good idea. We can select a variety of items, make a party of the trip. How long to get to San Diego?"

"Two days. I hope you'll be rested enough. That storm sounds exhausting."

"Thank goodness it hit us on the way there, rather than coming back. I'll be fine, Ian. I'm not too tired at all."

"You're sure?" he asked eagerly.

"Particularly not for that," Rebecca responded with an impish grin.

Rebecca and Ian lay in each other's arms. Their lovemaking had been good, lasting two wonderful, yet exhausting hours. Both tingled with slowly subsiding sensations of delightful stimulation, enjoying the crisp, cool breeze that blew in through the window of Rebecca's room. Although they continued to discover new things about each other, every nuance of their erotic gambits seemed comfortable and familiar, like the feel of a long-owned coat.

"You're none the worse for wear," Ian remarked casually, his hands exploring her body in a wonderfully amorous way.

"I could take that as an insult," Rebecca answered in a dreamy tone. "But I won't. You're the same, too. Only better, always and every time, better."

"My, what a fount of compliments you are tonight," Ian teased.

"Enjoy it while you can. When we locate Roger there won't be time for . . . this."

"And why not?"

"Too busy chasing them, trying to corner Roger."

Ian tensed, his voice changed harshly. "So you can kill him, as well?"

"If necessary. What's . . . the matter, Ian?"

"Even if my spirit isn't strong when it comes to the matter of our love, I still am a minister of the Gospel. Murder is a mortal sin. I can't condone your having it on your soul."

"Ian, it's *my* soul. Not to worry, dearest. Let's not dwell on what hasn't happened as yet. I'm more interested in this impudent spirit that keeps poking me in the belly. Any suggestions as to what to do with it?"

"As a matter of fact . . ."

A brief second later, Rebecca squealed in delight. "Oh, yes. What a wonderful idea. And, yes, that's good, too. And . . . that . . . OOOH . . . THAT IS SO GOOD!"

Gone for the night, all worries turned to sweetness.

Chapter 14

Tall, craggy peaks surrounded the heavy coach. Boulders, which looked to be poised upon hope alone, hung precariously over the narrow trail. Campo, with its small army post, stone store, and blacksmith shop had been left long behind. Here and there, the brush huts of Diegueño families dotted the less extreme valley slopes. Cattle roamed wild on open range. Cactus, manzanita, and yucca provided ground cover, with the uniform gold of seared grass as a carpet over the pale red-brown soil. Dust boiled up from the wheels. The rattle and slam made conversation all but impossible.

"Not far now, folks," the driver called out jovially. "We've entered Rancho Jamul. Two more stops for horses and we'll be at the depot in San Diego."

"Oh," Hester exclaimed. "Then these aren't real wild cattle?"

"They belong to someone, dear," Ian explained. "Look at the brand they wear." He pointed to a design on the flanks of the grazing creatures that resembled a double ox bow over a heart.

"Have you picked a hotel?" Hester inquired.

"Not likely. Though the manager at Julian said the best place in New Town was the Horton House. In Old

Town the Casa de Bandini."

"I do hope they're not dreary old places. How far would it be from San Diego to Los Vallecitos de San Marcos Rancho?"

Rebecca and Ian exchanged conspiratorial grins. "Too far for an afternoon's visit, my dear," Ian told her.

"Besides, who do you know who might be there to visit?"

"Oh, Rebecca, you know exactly whom I want to see."

"Manuel, is it? And how is it you learned so much about his little home in the north?"

"You're teasing me. I won't tolerate this another moment. Oh . . . how I wish . . ."

"That Manuel was riding shotgun guard so you'd have someone to defend your honor?" Ian added in, enjoying the pestering.

"I don't need Manuel for that," Hester snapped, faintly irritated by the game her elders played. "Lone Wolf will do quite well, thank you."

"That's right," the lanky, curly-haired blond Crow warrior spoke up with a leer. "Come sit in my lap and I'll protect you."

"Ooooh! You're all terrible. I'll . . . I'll find me a handsome ship's officer in San Diego and . . . sail away to paradise with him. You'll see."

"Not so fast, young lady," Ian demanded, suddenly caught up in more than he had foreseen.

"There," Hester responded archly. "Now the shoe's on the other foot, and it pinches, doesn't it, brother dear?"

Ian could only look sheepish.

Down in the lower valleys, the travelers observed lush fields, stately orchards of apples, apricots, and figs. Well-tended vineyards mottled the hillsides and orange groves marched along the wide, well-used roads. Most of the agricultural work was done by Mexican and Indian laborers. Their white cotton trousers and shirts and brown straw sombreros dotted the abundant acreages. Already the sharp tang of salt air tingled in their nostrils.

"What's that I smell?" Hester asked with scant tact.

"Sea air," Ian informed her. "We can't be more than twelve miles from the ocean, as the crow flies."

"San Diego in one hour," the driver called down.

"I can hardly wait," Hester enthused. "Is it really an old city?"

"Not so old as Santa Fe," Rebecca Caldwell told her. "The oldest in California, though."

With the improvement in the roads, light conversation was once again possible. The four occupants of the coach passed the time pleasantly. When the first buildings of the bustling New Town appeared, the mood changed abruptly.

"I wonder where Roger Styles has his office?" Rebecca questioned aloud.

"If he's here, we'll find him," Lone Wolf assured her.

Bright blue sky above, the heady aroma of the bay, and wheeling, screeching gulls set the stage for their arrival at the Butterfield depot. A flock of small boys hovered about, vying to carry luggage in return for a small reward. Ian and Lone Wolf selected several and indicated their belongings.

"Take them to the Horton House," the minister instructed. "If anything's missing, my friend and I will warm the bottoms of your trousers."

Reeling under the weight of Hester's copious equipage, the youngsters hurried away. At a more leisurely pace, the quartet started up Broad Street toward the small central plaza. To the eyes of those accustomed to open spaces and an unhurried pace, people appeared to move about frenetically. Twice men with their heads down and hands holding bowlers in place on them bumped into Rebecca and sped past with only a muttered word of apology.

"It's all so . . . hurried," Rebecca remarked to her companions.

"And so big," Hester added.

"Where do we start?"

"At our hotel, I'd suggest," Lone Wolf offered.

"Good idea. Roger had to stay somewhere when he came here."

"Don't get your hopes up too high, Becky," Ian cautioned.

"Four rooms for five nights each," the youthful desk clerk at the Horton House said crisply. "That'll be thirty dollars total." He rapped a silver-domed bell and called in a peremptory voice. "Front, boy!"

After settling in, Rebecca met her companions in the airy, sunlit tearoom off the main dining room. They ordered light refreshments and set to work dividing up the chores necessary to locating information on Roger Styles. Rebecca outlined her proposal and conversation halted while a uniformed waiter brought their snack and richly aromatic coffee.

"Hester, I think you'd be best suited for charming any knowledge out of our desk clerk and the bellboys. You work on that. Lone Wolf and Ian can check the dock area. Knowing Roger, I'm sure he acquired a number of unsavory characters to back him up. Obviously so, if he's responsible for these attacks on the Indian villages. I'll talk with the businessmen."

Ian frowned slightly, hesitant to broach the subject with Rebecca. "Uh, Becky, most businessmen consider their affairs to be the province of males only. I'm not so certain you'll receive any sort of cordial reception."

"Why, that's ridiculous. A woman has every right to make inquiries."

132

"Not the way some see it," Ian pressed.

Rebecca's face changed, smoothing into bland, helpless innocence. "What man could refuse to assist a young widow, seeking advice on how to wisely invest the funds her late husband left her? After all, poor little me hasn't any kind of head for business. I only want to do what's right. And there's talk of this simply clever fellow, Roger Styles, who is open to investment in his latest project."

"Great Spirit help us!" Lone Wolf exclaimed in a shout of laughter. "You do that well enough to almost have me believing it, Rebecca."

"Thank you, kind sir."

"I think you might get away with it," Ian agreed with a kind of wonder.

Early afternoon found them diligently pursuing their assigned tasks. Hester totally charmed the young desk clerk. He could not take his eyes from her and he tugged frequently at the high, starched collar of his shirt, as though steam might be building up below it. Hester found him handsome and dashing. Not heroic like Manuel, who had saved her life, but interesting. It took her little time to loosen his tongue.

"Yes, we had had a Roger Styles staying at the hotel some three weeks ago, for four days, I believe it was."

"Do you know where he might have gone from here, Daniel?"

"No, no idea where he went. He, ah, looked down on the hotel staff as menials, Hester. Would there be anything else I can help with?"

Hester batted her eyes and gave him the sweetest of her smiles. "Why, yes, there is. Do you by any means recall any of his associates during that time?"

"Uh . . . Mr. Horton, of course. And Frank Kimball. He seemed to be known by all the important people in town."

"Thank you ever so much. You've been so kind to me."

"Do you mind . . . uh, could you, that is, tell me why it is you wanted to know this?"

"We're trying to find Mr. Styles. A business matter."

"I've heard he's left town. For where I don't know."

"Thank you again, Daniel. You've been so sweet to help me like this." Hester departed, quite proud of herself.

Rebecca inquired after Roger at three banks before she came up with any solid information.

"Mr. Styles? Umm, yes. He had an account here. At least during the time he engaged in some transactions with another gentleman."

"Who would that be?"

"I'm, ah, not at liberty to say. However, I can tell you that the other gentleman has returned to his homeland, in Russia."

"Was this a private venture for Mr. Styles?"

"Yes, that deal, at least. When he first opened his account with us, he was associated with New Town Development Corporation. That's, ah, Alonzo Horton."

"I see. Thank you very much. Did he have any other associates?"

The pudgy banker shrugged. "Who needs other partners when one is in business with Alonzo Horton?"

Rebecca asked directions to the offices of New Town Development and departed. When she arrived there, she met her first real obstacle.

"I'm sorry, miss, but Mister Horton is not seeing anyone today," the prissy secretary informed her. "Could I take your name and arrange for an appointment tomorrow or the next day?"

"This is terribly important," Rebecca urged. "It would only take a minute."

134

"Mr. Horton is not in the office. Otherwise . . ." the clerkish young man shrugged thin shoulders, "something might be worked out."

"I . . . see. Thank you all the same. I'm Rebecca Caldwell and I'm staying at the Horton House. Tomorrow anytime would be fine. It's regarding a Mr. Roger Styles."

The secretary's eyebrows raised to peaks at mention of the name, though he managed to maintain a straight face. He made a notation on a slip of paper and opened a small, black leather-bound appointment book.

"Would two-thirty tomorrow afternoon be all right?"

"Yes, of course."

"Very well then. Good day."

Rebecca went next to the city building to talk with the chief of police. A white-haired, mustachioed gentleman of Mexican extraction ushered her into his office and inquired as to the reason for her visit.

"Chief Vasquez, I'm trying to gather information regarding a man named Roger Styles."

"Ah, yes, that scoundrel. Alonzo Horton and Sheriff Hunsaker sent him packing, with my blessing, let me add."

"Oh, then, his real nature became known?"

"You might say that." Vasquez's dark black eyes narrowed. "I gather that you know quite a bit about Roger Styles, Miss, ah, Caldwell?"

"Probably a great deal more than anyone in San Diego. What I don't know is what he has been up to since he came here."

"He has a checkered past?"

"Quite so. He's a wanted criminal in seven states and three territories."

"Confidence schemes, most likely," the old lawman said authoritatively.

"Among other things, including murder, arson,

grand theft and white slaving."

"My, he's a busy man, our Roger Styles. Where do you figure into this?"

Rebecca took a deep breath and readied herself for the inevitable ordeal. "I've been trying to bring an end to his evil career."

"An admirable pursuit for anyone. Yet, one would think that a lovely young woman would find better use of her time."

"In the kitchen, with kiddies running around and a husband to care for? Oh, I've heard it all, a thousand times over. Let me tell you about Roger Styles."

For twenty minutes, Rebecca related her unforgettable tale of privation and despair, sprinkled with highlights of cornering members of the Tulley Gang and those who had aided them. Chief Vasquez shook his head in sympathy and astonishment. At last he brushed at the flowing sides of his mustache with the back of one index finger and cleared his throat.

"It's good riddance for San Diego to have this villain gone, I daresay."

"Do you have any idea where he might have headed?"

"Ummm. There are some say he has carved out a small empire for himself in the mountainous portion of Rancho Jamul. I can't say for sure on that. You might talk to the sheriff or Mr. Horton regarding the actual situation."

"Thank you, I shall. I have an appointment with Mr. Horton for tomorrow afternoon."

"With luck, by that time he might not be too busy to see you," Vasquez said wryly.

"Why do you say that?"

"Alonzo means well. It's only that he has a great many more demands on his time than he has hours in the day."

"I can be most persuasive, Chief Vasquez."

"That I believe wholeheartedly. Well then, I wish you well."

"Is there anything more you can tell me?"

"Not really. Except Roger Styles did do the city a favor."

"How's that?"

"He hired more'n half the riffraff and low-lifes down along the harbor. They all left town with him."

"That doesn't sound too promising."

"Not if you intend to face him man-to-ah, er, man."

A trill of laughter came from Rebecca's lovely lips. "When I started out this afternoon, I was warned that I would find it to be very much a man's world. I never gave thought to how that fact influences even our mode of speech. Thank you for your concern, Chief Vasquez. But I've been shot at and missed and shot at and hit several times before. And I've probably killed more men in the last two years than you have in your entire career in law enforcement. I won't go after Roger alone, and I have no intention to try to stand against impossible odds. Time's my best ally."

"How do you mean that?"

"I have a lot of it and Roger doesn't. Every day I get a little closer."

"You've got a lot of spunk, Miss Caldwell."

Rebecca rose and they said their good-byes. After she departed, Chief Vasquez spoke aloud to himself the thoughts he had not dared to express in her presence.

"I sure as hell wouldn't want that gal after me."

When she returned to the hotel, Rebecca was given a stiff white card from her pigeon hole behind the counter. "*Regret to inform you Mr. Horton unavoidably delayed. Will not return to San Diego until Thursday. I have taken the liberty to reset your appointment for the same time that*

The chief of police had been right on that one, Rebecca thought with disappointment. She assembled with the others and they compared the results of their afternoon. When the last report had been made, Rebecca reached a conclusion.

"It seems to me the next thing on hand is to get a look at Rancho Jamul. We rode right through the middle of it on the way here, didn't we?"

"That's right."

"If we'd only known," Rebecca said wistfully. "Anyway, someone should scout out that place."

"I'll be happy to," Lone Wolf volunteered, rising. "But first, I want a steak and one of those sweet-tasting abalone."

"No great hurry," Rebecca informed him. "I think we'll join you in that. What about tomorrow, Ian?"

"Not given it much thought. What about a ride around to see the bay?"

"A wonderful idea. Shall we go in to eat?"

Chapter 15

A rattle of wheels rose from the street in front of the Horton House. The low coastal fog had yet to burn away, so that the sun appeared as a milk-white dime high in the swirling mist. People swarmed the walks and construction noises came from several building sites. By midmorning, Lone Wolf had not returned from his scouting mission. Breakfast over, Hester made ready to depart with the young desk clerk, whose day off it was. They planned to take in the "quaint" sights of Old Town and visit the historic spots. Ian Claymore had a carriage brought and suggested that he and Rebecca Caldwell travel westward around the bay and learn more about the land.

Rebecca agreed and excused herself. In the spacious kitchen she consulted with the chef.

"Do you have a large hamper? Something suitable to hold a picnic lunch?"

"Oh, yes, miss. We have an ample supply. We get frequent calls for such. What is it you desire?"

Rebecca considered the issue. "Some cold ham, cheeses, a dozen fresh oysters, bread, and boiled eggs will do nicely."

"What about a nice shrimp remoulade? The catch

was brought in before dawn this morning. Also two bottles of fine San Pasquale wine, a claret, and a tart young sauterne?"

Clapping her hands in delight, Rebecca agreed to it all.

"Half an hour and it will be ready, miss."

"Excellent. Have it brought to our carriage. It'll be waiting out front."

"As you wish, miss."

Rebecca returned to her room in high spirits. What should she wear? She searched her belongings. Definitely the high-topped moccasins favored by the desert-dwelling tribes. There were bound to be rough grasses and burrs in the strange country they would visit. Her riding habit? No. Too stiff and formal, to say nothing of the material becoming a haven for foxtails and other annoyances. She had a soft leather skirt, purchased in Julian. Ideal. The blouse to her riding outfit? A bit frilly, but it would serve. In twenty minutes time she had dressed and come down to the lobby. Ian met her there.

"You look lovely."

"Why, thank you, Ian. You're quite the dandy yourself."

Ian wore a moderate style of the popular Mexican *ranchero* costume. Tight-fitting trousers, though without the silver conchos and red inletted gussets, complemented a cummerbund of darker brown, a frilly white shirt, and a bolero jacket. A flat-crowned Cordoban sombrero topped it off. Around his waist he wore a hand-tooled leather holster, which contained his .44 Remington revolver. His low boots were shiny and new. He patted the gun scabbard, almost by way of apology.

"I was told that where we're going there are a lot of rattlesnakes." He blushed slightly when he recalled her shooting off the head of a sidewinder on the desert.

"You look capable of handling them," Rebecca replied firmly. "I ordered us a lunch. It should be ready anytime now."

"Wonderful. There's a good trail around the north end of the bay that leads to the top of Point Loma and the Spanish lighthouse there. My informants say it's the most spectacular view of San Diego from that spot. Then I thought we'd go on to Playa del Mar, though a lot of local Anglos are starting to call it Ocean Beach."

Through an admiring grin, Rebecca said, "You've learned a lot of local geography in a short time."

"Claymore's Friendly Guide Service at your command, ma'am. Ah! Looks like our viands coming now."

Shortly after ten-thirty Ian drove the sprightly carriage away from the crumbled old walls of the first Presidio of San Diego and headed west, around the curving end of the bay. At his side, Rebecca breathed deeply of the crisp salt air and marveled at the large collection of seagoing vessels at anchor in the harbor.

"I've only once been on a big ship," Rebecca confided, recalling her passage from New Orleans to Galveston. "It was quite exhilarating. Particularly when we encountered a gigantic storm at sea. A hurricane, the captain told us."

Ian scowled briefly. "Not many vessels survive those tempests. You were fortunate. When was this?"

"A little over a year and a half ago."

"You were chasing Roger Styles, no doubt."

"Yes. All the way through Texas, as it turned out."

The topic, so suddenly exposed to the light, put a pall on the conversation for several minutes. Then Rebecca partly rose from her seat and pointed toward the water. Excitement shone in her deep blue eyes.

"Look! Look over there, Ian. Aren't they marvelous?"

Four ponderous pelicans rode the gentle roll in the bay. In no discernible order of preference, one would muster up sufficient speed to lift its ungainly body from the surface and flop around in a circle, hover, then dive into the blue-green bay. It would emerge moments later with water sieving from its distended beak pouch, which wriggled with a generous catch of small fish.

Its meal secured for the moment, the creature would rest while another of its brothers repeated the process. From the number of dives, Rebecca decided that the birds must require an enormous amount to nourish themselves. Their pace slowed then, as the carriage started into the long, uphill pull to the top of the fingerlike projection called Point Loma.

Deputy Federal Land Commissioner Matthew Wheaton sat across the wide expanse of highly polished table in the formal dining room of Casa Rogelio. He drank fine brandy from a cut crystal goblet and smiled satisfactorily at his host. Roger Styles returned the gesture with a suggestive smirk.

"You find everything in order, Mr. Commissioner?"

"I certainly do," Wheaton responded boisterously.

His mind dwelled on the fifteen thousand dollars in cash tucked away in an inside pocket of his coat. He gave no thought to the small bank draft for purchase of certain lands, held in supposed "perpetual reserve for the tribes collectively known by the nominative Diegueño." Twenty-five thousand six hundred acres, forty square miles, transferred to the Casa Rogelio Land Company for the niggardly sum of ten cents an acre, made a tidy package. One well worth the generous gratuity he had received. Of course, he'd have to give two thousand to the title clerk who had helped ease the transaction. What of it? Thirteen thousand made a suitable reward. He cleared his throat before asking for the usual assurance.

"Naturally, my name will never be connected to this deal, eh? After all, among gentlemen . . ."

"Such unpleasantries need never be mentioned, Mr. Commissioner. Will you stay over for the fiesta tonight?"

"I, ah, I'm afraid not. Must get back to Los Angeles, you know. I'd certainly enjoy it," Wheaton concluded wistfully.

A sheen of perspiration broke out on his large forehead and along the edge of his receding hairline. Only too well he recalled the energetic gyrations of the lithe young Mexican girl who had shared his bed the previous night. She'd wrung him dry, long before either of them desired sleep. Even then, he'd managed to keep it up and receive waves of unfettered rapture beyond anything he had ever experienced in life or fantasy.

Roger slid back his chair and captured his commissioner's attention once more. "Well then, that concludes our little business. Before you go, I might mention that there's another parcel of land I'm interested in. From what I hear, there are no Indians occupying it any longer. As such, it has reverted to your department's jurisdiction. Perhaps you could look into it for me?"

"Uh . . . well, I . . . are you *sure* there are no savages in the area?"

Roger produced a wicked, wolfish grin. "Let's say I'm positive of it. Our, ah, arrangements would be the same, if that's satisfactory to you."

"Oh, indeed, indeed. Only, I'd urge caution. Too much too soon might attract the attention of my superiors."

"Very well, then." Roger rose and indicated the

french windows that led to the inner courtyard. "I would like to proceed on this new claim within, say, two weeks."

"So soon? It could be done, I suppose."

"What if another development company happened to bid on it?"

Wheaton considered this a moment, then affected a scowl of disapproval, the reaction he anticipated his host desired. "I'm afraid their offer would be unsuitable, in light of your own."

"I was thinking of South Bay Development Corporation. A company wholly owned by me. Yet not the same one to make this initial purchase."

A beaming smile lighted Wheaton's face. "Brilliant. A marvelous idea, sir. Under the circumstances, I think I can assure there would be no insurmountable difficulties."

"Excellent. I'll contact you when we're ready to proceed. Have a safe trip, Mr. Commissioner."

Fine as milled wheat flour, a bluish haze hung over the heaving expanse of the Pacific Ocean. Closer to shore, where the surf broke on the land, minute particles of red-brown sand joined the mist. A steady hissing came from the combing edges of the breakers, followed by the rumble and retreat of the mighty waves. Rebecca Caldwell stood watching it in awe. The sea air made her tingle with excitement. Bright-eyed, she turned to Ian Claymore.

"Can we walk in the water's edge?"

"If you wish."

"It's beautiful. Yet, all so powerful."

"And it's called the *peaceful* ocean," Ian remarked.

"Let me take off my moccasins," Rebecca urged. "You can get out of your boots and leave them here with the blanket and our picnic things."

"Right enough. Only what do I do with my new trousers?"

"Roll the legs up. Or . . . take them off," Rebecca suggested as she studied the vast expanse of empty beach. "There's no one here but us."

Ian saw the hungry look of passion in her eyes and grinned. "That's a marvelous idea. Let's both get out of our clothes and take a splash."

Quickly they disrobed and ran like children to the water's edge. Rebecca stepped in up to her knees.

"It's so warm!" she cried in surprise.

"Compared to a mountain stream, you're right," Ian agreed.

A big breaker came in and splashed them to their shoulders. "Oh, Ian, it's wonderful."

For the next twenty minutes they let the surf pound them, often diving through a seven-foot wall of water to come out gasping and laughing on the other side. The incoming tide toyed with them, increasing their enjoyment. Finally, one huge breaker crashed down and drove them into each other's arms. Rebecca squealed with delight as they struggled against the strong undertow. Their bodies pressed tighter together and they felt a new warmth radiating from deep within. Neither of the young lovers needed words to decide their actions.

His hand in hers, Ian led Rebecca partway up the incline of wet sand. They sank to their knees in a gentle wash of water. There they embraced.

When the kiss ended, Rebecca whispered softly in Ian's ear. "I love you, Ian."

"And I love you, Becky."

Slowly at first, then with mounting energy, their hands explored each other's body. Their ardor grew while the sun prickled their skin in time with the tingling of their mounting fervor. Rebecca moaned and caressed Ian's muscular flesh. In expanding frenzy, she kissed her way down his broad chest and hard, flat belly.

"Yes," Ian sighed softly. "Oh, yes."

Rebecca increased the pressure of her lips and tongue, thrilling to the sweet taste of Ian's body, then flung herself back on the wet, hard-packed sand. The waves curled around her gloriously bronze form, etching her in bold relief. Ian came to her, splashing on his knees. Slowly he lowered herself between her inviting thighs.

Shivers of ecstasy ran through Rebecca's slender body when Ian penetrated her. The warmth of sun, sand and sea enveloped her in nature's tender embrace. She shivered in delight and raked her fingernails along his spine. Ian shuddered and pierced her to the ultimate. There they clung, on the precipice over ultimate oblivion, each surging with the longing to make this magic moment last an eternity.

"Ian!" Rebecca gasped. "Oh, now, Ian!"

Grunts and cries of passion rose from each ecstatic partner, in such volume and profusion that they startled the gulls. The black-gray-and-white creatures skreed and wheeled away in alarm. The next wave washed over them both, adding a new and wonderful zest to their coupling. With increasing strength and speed, Ian thrust away in a whirlwind of urgency. Abruptly, as they neared the peak, their world of euphoria disintegrated around them.

"Are you guys fightin'?" a small soprano voice inquired.

"Naw, dummy. They're doin' what my Pop calls 'makin' the beast with two backs,' " came a piping reply.

"You mean . . . they're DOIN' IT?" the first blurted.

"Ye-ep," his companion dragged out, eyes alight with interest.

146

Rebecca and Ian came startled back into reality to see two totally naked little boys of ten or eleven standing near to them. Both freckled lads whispered and giggled at what they had witnessed, then whirled and ran away.

"Ohmygod!" Rebecca gulped.

"Rather shattering, wasn't it," Ian agreed.

"What are they doing here?" Rebecca demanded in a fluster.

"They're going fishing, I'd imagine," Ian answered, pointing to the folded net held between the sun-browned boys. "They must come here often. Probably live somewhere close by. They'd have left their clothes up on the grassy bank, like we did."

"Why'd they have to pick today?" Rebecca queried wretchedly. She looked about her in confusion. "What shall we . . . what *can* we do now?"

"I'd suggest," Ian offered dryly, "that we wash off the sand, dress ourselves, and proceed with our picnic."

Surprising Ian, Rebecca flushed a bright pink from the roots of her jet-black hair to the tips of her toes. "How can we . . . possibly . . . after what we . . . I mean after what they . . . saw . . . and . . . all?"

"Why not? From the looks of them, from their giggles, they obviously approved. Nasty little buggers, it'll give 'em foul dreams for weeks. C'mon, my love, up you go. Let's get the sand off and go on like nothing untoward happened."

"Ian . . . sometimes you shock me beyond . . . beyond. Oh, all right. I suppose putting the best possible face on it is the right course."

Sunlight slanted long and orange across the bay, bringing out sandpipers and coots to search for vulnerable shellfish buried in the tidal flats. Rebecca and Ian, flushed and burned by sun, salt, spray, and wind,

147

clattered into San Diego's New Town in the hush that preceded sundown. Ian left the carriage with a stable boy at the Horton House, and they entered the hotel. A note waited in Rebecca's box.

"Oh, not again. I won't countenance another delay."

"There you are, Miss Caldwell. This message came from Mr. Horton's office."

"I feared as much," Rebecca answered the desk clerk, expecting the worst.

She opened it and read, her features enlivening with each word. When she put it aside, she clasped one of Ian's strong hands in her own. Highlights danced in her eyes.

"It's good news, Ian. I've been invited, along with my associates, to attend upon Mr. Alonzo Horton, at his residence, tonight at seven o'clock. Dress to be formal. Isn't that wonderful?"

"It is, indeed. Except that gives us less than an hour and a quarter to clean up, change and get there."

"We'll do it," Rebecca returned confidently. "This is one summons I have no intention of refusing."

Chapter 16

Soft music tinkled from the pianoforte in one corner of the large solarium of Alonzo Hoton's mansion. Played by his lovely eldest daughter, the popular songs of the time still had a discordant sound to Rebecca Caldwell's ears. Accustomed to Sioux flutes, rattles, and drums, the octave scale jarred her musical sense. She sat in a love seat, with Ian Claymore at her side, Alonzo Horton opposite on a chair. The ruggedly good-looking financier retained a startled expression at the conclusion of Rebecca's discourse on Roger Styles.

"I must say I'm amazed by all this, Miss Caldwell. It's far more distressing than I expected. If you'll pardon my coarse language, I should have had the bastard hanged."

"Oh, but that would have deprived me of the chance to get revenge," Rebecca replied sweetly. Ian scowled.

"Young lady, let me presume upon age to make it clear to you that I can discern a fighter when I see one. I harbor no doubt as to your prowess. Not even when I see you in that lovely dress."

"You're a flatterer, Mr. Horton."

"Alonzo to you, my dear. Let me continue. You say that your companion is scouting the suspected headquarters of Roger's present operation. If he determines that that scoundrel is indeed at Rancho Jamul, Sheriff Hunsaker should be apprised of it immediately. Wherever he is, Styles has some sixty to seventy brawlers and hardcases with him. Hardly what you could face alone. At the present, there's little that can be done officially, however."

"Why is that?"

"Styles is not wanted for anything in California. Unless and until it can be proven he is behind these attacks on Indian communities in San Diego County, there's nothing the sheriff can do. I'm sorry my dear." The crafty businessman paused as though caught on a stray thought.

"Of course, if you and your companions can do something about that. . . "

"I'd like nothing better, Alonzo."

"Good, good. Now, let me refresh that sherry for you."

"Only a little one, please. I'm not accustomed to strong drink. The truth is, this has made me a bit tiddly."

Alonzo chuckled and patted her hand. "Have no fear. Dinner will be along soon. Then you'll hardly know you have consumed a thing."

"If I may, Alonzo, what exactly can the sheriff do against so many, if you feel we would not prevail?"

"He can organize a posse. Deputize every able man in town, if need be. There are cannon on some of my ships in port. They can be dismounted and hauled in wagons. Such a force would be formidable."

"How long would all that take?"

"Oh, a day or so, another day to move into position."

"Then perhaps we should do what we can and call for help when we need it."

"You're as stubborn as you are beautiful. Can't I

dissuade you somehow?"

"Sorry, but no, Alonzo. When Lone Wolf returns, we'll talk with the sheriff. Beyond that, I can't promise much."

Glowing a soft red, like the sun through a desert sand storm, a light hung before Alberto Rosas's eyes. What could it be? Why did he try to cringe away from it? Then his fogged mind recalled and he screamed.

"It's going to be easy," Roger Styles gloated. "I didn't even touch him and he bellowed like a castrated bull. Let's see what a taste of it on his hide will elicit?"

Stretched naked across a refectory table, bound hand and foot, Alberto Rosas's coppery skin glistened with a slime of fear sweat. He fought against his bonds in an attempt to evade the cherry-hued poker in Roger's hands. A sizzling sound came when his tormentor pressed the heated metal into flesh an inch below Alberto's right nipple.

Sickly sweet, the odor of burned human tissue rose from the table. Alberto arched his back, a howl torn from his bloody, pulped mouth. Then he went slackly into unconsciousness. Roger removed the poker.

"Water, Miguel. It seems the poor savage has fled from us. This time I think I shall use . . . the tongs."

A figure moved in the darkness, away from the brightly lighted torture theatre. Dooley Walsh cleared thick phlegm from his throat and spat it out in a gesture of disgust. He wiped his face with a neckerchief.

"Somehow, Roger, this torture crap goes against the grain. I ain't a'feared of any man, with fist, knife, or gun. But a helpless dumb thing like that, burned and cut and slashed, it . . . it ain't civilized."

"Don't fret yourself, Dooley. You don't have to stay and watch, you know."

151

Walsh brightened. Being *segundo* to Roger Styles had been all right so far, but the tormenting of these poor Indians stuck in his craw. He nodded then and licked dry lips.

"In that case, I think I'll go make the rounds, see the boys are alert on guard duty. We ridin' out again tomorrow?"

"No. We wouldn't have time. Day after that, Rudolfo Mateo is bringing an important man for a conference on joining forces. With the addition of his men, there's no force in California large enough to stop us. I'm looking forward to it."

"Well an' good, then, Roger. I'll see you in the morning."

"Not joining me for a brandy before turning in?"

"I'll pass this time, thanks all the same. Good night."

"Good night. Oh, Dooley, have Uvaldo send . . . ah, Carmensita, I think . . . yes, have Carmensita sent to my room. This sort of work always makes me feel lusty."

"I'll see to it, Roger."

The moment he left the torture chamber in the old adobe barn, an expression of disgust twisted Dooley Walsh's face. Lusty all right, he thought in contempt. Damned right. He could tell that Roger was already aroused. Dooley had noticed this phenomenon before, and revolted though he was, he found himself fascinated by it. It was as though Roger might be shy a few cards in his deck. Gettin' all worked up over blood and pain. That he called plain sick. Dooley headed to the main house to give Uvaldo his instructions.

That was another thing that annoyed Dooley about his boss. Carmensita couldn't be more than fourteen. Granted, he'd hankered after the young stuff more than once in his life. Mostly when he was young himself. Seemed, though, that Roger wouldn't have it any other way. And they all came away with welts and bruises. Downright sick.

Back in the barn, Roger turned to his thankless task.

"Come now, you're going to tell me. Might as well be now. Miguel, ask him the names of his people who are willing to fight back."

Miguel Beltran rattled off rapid-fire Spanish. The young Diegueño moaned, then answered in a weak voice.

"He says you are a coward who murders children and hides behind an adobe wall. I'm sorry, *patrón*, but that is what he says."

Roger crossed rapidly to the table. His hand lashed out at the already bruised and battered man. The Indian howled. A twisted smile writhed beneath the pencil line of Roger's newly grown mustache.

"This is how I reward insolence. Tell him, Miguel."

Stubbornly, Alberto Rosas refused to make coherent reply. Roger seized the tongs. He snapped the pincers closed over Rosas's flesh with a finality that generated more thrashing and shrieks of agony from his victim. Panting, Roger realized that he was beginning to enjoy himself. He released the cooling tongs and sought a new instrument.

"*Exinnk. Exinnk. Ammai Kwirak, Amat Sinye, mesxapulyii minyawaptc. Exinnk,*" the courageous Alberto chanted.

"What's he saying?"

"It is one. It is one. Sky Father, Earth mother, I fly to you. It is one.' It's his death song."

Before Roger could react, the young man simply stopped breathing and let the life flee from his body. "Damn!" Roger exploded. "Oh, damn, damn, damn. He escaped from me. That's ruined everything. Get him out of here. Take him!" he shrieked at Miguel. "Leave me here alone for a while."

Feeling daunted, defeated by a mere savage, Roger vented his fury by smashing a terracotta water pitcher, hurling the fragment against the wall and crying great, salty tears. His fury spent, he started off for the main house, thoughts of the tender flesh of young Carmensita fresh in his mind.

Chapter 17

Daybreak, usually a welcome time to most people, is a dubious friend to someone scouting an enemy. With the coming of light comes increased danger. During the night, Lone Wolf had managed to work in close to the headquarters of Roger Styles's operation at Rancho Jamul. His problem now lay in getting away unseen. He crouched in a cluster of boulders, shielded from above by the gnarled limbs of a large and ancient oak. Voices came clearly to him from beyond the low wall being enlarged around the hacienda.

"Nevah had ever'one heah at one time lak this," a voice declared in a lazy Down East nasal drawl.

"Boss wants to put on a big show fer this Mezkin I suppose," a companion opined.

"A-yap. Though I don't see the need, them bein' Papists an' the like. 'Twas me doin' the thinkin' we'd have no truck with their sort."

"Maybe that's why Roger's the boss an' you're just another fast gun."

"You could be right, Ab." He yawned and stretched, his head and arms showing above the incomplete wall. "Nigh onto time for our relief. I could stand some breakfast."

Heartbeats counted time for Lone Wolf for some five minutes. The sentries had lapsed into silence, though the awakening sounds of a new day came from other parts of the rancho. A cock crowed defiantly. Horses snorted and stomped in the corral. Wood smoke rose from the chimney of the cookshack. The first insects of the day shift took to the air, buzzing and flitting around.

"Cleveland, Stocker, you can head on in now. We'll be takin' yer place," another man hailed.

"An' about time, I figah," the Vermonter snapped.

The whole gang in one place, Lone Wolf considered. He'd counted the arrival of some thirty riders during the hours before midnight. There'd been talk in town of Roger's having more than sixty men under his command. A formidable force by any reckoning. Rebecca had been right, he considered ruefully. Whatever Styles had in mind, he'd gathered enough guns to make sure he got his way. If only some way could be devised to attack while all of Roger's strength was inside those walls. Trapped like that, they could be easy prey. A more pressing problem reasserted itself.

Would he have to wait until nightfall to get away from the area safely? Sentries, although sloppy in the performance of their duties, watched constantly. And what about this Mexican the guards had been discussing? Who was he and of what importance? A desperate plan began to form in his mind.

Only one man would recognize him. Roger Styles. Could he, Lone Wolf pondered, appear on a back trail and ride in as a straggler? Not all of the sixty men could have reported by now. It should be easy. A force that size provided ample cover. Another anonymous face in a crowd. So long as Roger never got a close look, he might be able to pull it off. The problem would be in getting to where he had left his horse, then circling around the hacienda so that he could come in from the east. The thought became action as the newly stationed guards turned inward to watch the rowdy clutter of two score men spill from several buildings and head toward the aroma of cooking food.

The first hundred yards held the most danger. Bent low, Lone Wolf zigzagged through the grass, seeking what protection the manzanita and sage clumps could offer.

Think like a rabbit, he told himself. You're small and frightened and seeking to avoid the sharp eye of that big red-tail hawk up there. Move in spurts, dart from place to place. After years of practice, the Crow method of deceiving any prying eyes while hunting a prey came naturally to Lone Wolf. No alarm came by the time he reached his goal.

In a cluster of mixed trees he retrieved his horse and started away from the hacienda, up a narrow, twisting canyon that led northeast. His next danger point would come when he climbed to the saddle that rose high and treeless above the ravine. The ascent would take him a good hour. Barring rattlesnakes, he'd be all right until then. The volume of noise rose from down below. Sufficient, he felt, to cover any he made.

For the first quarter of a mile, everything went as Lone Wolf anticipated. It would have continued to do so if it hadn't been for the crows. Two of the large, black birds took up a complaining clack, cawing stridently and bouncing up and down on gray limbs of an old, dead tree. Lone Wolf halted instantly. He'd been seen. Their alarm would not fail to alert the sentries below. Six more of the obsidian-hued creatures took up the dispute.

Hell, this could be worse than a rattler, Lone Wolf thought. The damned crows would fly over next and begin to circle him, point out his exact location. More of the noisy birds glided in on large wings, filling the blasted oak until it became a huge black ball. The crows seemed to be bobbing up and down, darting their heads into the central portion of the tree. It looked somehow familiar to Lone Wolf. Their cawing became louder, more strident and insistent. Suddenly a lone bird burst from inside the sphere of its angry fellows and streaked away. First singly, then in pairs, followed by clusters of five or six, the squawking black creatures darted after it. And, yeah, Lone Wolf recognized what he'd seen.

A crow trial. Some inattentive sentry or a bird who had violated the pecking order had been brought to task by its peers, found guilty and fled, driven from the flock forever. Those who remained behind began to quiet down. With a sigh of relief, Lone Wolf started onward.

"Damn," he muttered in a barely audible whisper, "that was too close."

Three-qaurters of the way up, the brush and trees began to thin out. Lone Wolf tensed, mindful of the alarm caused by the crows. Another sixty feet and he would be out in the open. Far behind and below, the buildings of the old hacienda looked like toys. Small dots moved from place to place like so many ants. None seemed to pay attention to the high saddle notch. Still the white Crow warrior waited, studying his enemy from afar, sharply attuned to any sign of excitement.

When none came after another fifteeen minutes, he moved out with a purposeful stride. Frequently glancing backward, his breathing labored by the steep climb, Lone Wolf kept track of movement around the hacienda. A hundred feet to go and so far no sign of anyone's noticing him.

Fifty feet covered and still he remained undetected.

A dozen short strides more and he'd nearly reached the notch. Only half a dozen paces. His horse snorted and reared back, nostrils quivering, ears pointed forward. An instant later, Lone Wolf heard the furious buzz of a healthy-sized set of rattles.

Lying atop a flat rock, the green-and-brown Pacific Coast rattler reached a third of its length into the air, head weaving, small gold eyes aglitter. Its tongue flicked in and out, taking sense impressions of its surroundings. The thin yellow lines that outlined the brown diamond markings could have been considered beautiful under better circumstances. Now they only seemed to emphasize the menace of the huge reptile. Conditioning and instinct sent Lone Wolf's hand toward the butt of his Colt revolver.

No! The thought jolted through his head. Carefully he eased backward. While he did, his left hand sought out the tomahawk at his waist, behind the wide pliable leather belt. Disturbed, the six-foot snake darted forward, not in a strike, but a feint. Lone Wolf took another backward step.

At once the scaly horror gathered itself and lanced out, mouth open wide, retractable fangs extended, venom dripping. Lone Wolf swung the tomahawk with the fullness of his might. A foot-long segment, with head attached, flew to his right. The remainder of the rattler flopped and writhed on the ground. Lone Wolf followed through quickly, locating the smaller portion and destroying the deadly triangular skull with a pair of blows from the 'hawk. Showing the whites of its eyes, his mount snorted and shied around, stamping nervously.

The scent of snake blood and the feral odor of the reptilian killer brought the sturdy beast close to panic. Lone Wolf stroked its arched neck and spoke softly, soothingly.

"There, there. He can't hurt you now. Easy, boy. Take it easy."

It took all of Lone Wolf's effort to get the horse walking again. They skirted the still-undulating corpse and quickly negotiated the notch onto the slope beyond. Damn, he could have done without that, Lone Wolf considered, thankful it had ended as it had. Now, to get on around to the road.

Another day had come and still Lone Wolf had not returned from his scouting trip to Rancho Jamul. Rebecca Caldwell began to feel a slight unease. Could something have happened? She sent for Juan Lachusa, anxious to discover what went on at Roger's supposed headquarters.

"Juan, I have a little job for one of your men," Rebecca told the young Diegueño when he entered her room twenty minutes after she'd summoned him.

"What is that?

"Lone Wolf hasn't returned. From the stories we've heard, there are a lot of men out there. Perhaps someone discovered him. I'd like you to have one of the warriors your chief sent along go to Jamul to find out."

Juan frowned slightly. "I think I'll send two. If someone as good as Lone Wolf got caught, there's no telling what might happen.

"Good thinking," Rebecca agreed. "Tell them to be very careful. If they should encounter Lone Wolf on the way back here already, they're to turn back and accompany him."

"They'll leave within the hour." Juan turned to go, paused and turned back. "I . . . uh, about that afternoon in the cave. I . . . I suppose you couldn't help but notice how it affected me . . . ?"

Rebecca laughed lightly. "Oh, my, no. Your reaction was rather, ah, prominent. The truth is, I was strongly affected, too. So much so that it was all I could do to keep from going into the back of the cave with you."

Juan swallowed with difficulty. He took a hesitant step toward Rebecca, hands out in a gesture of supplication. In three swift strides, Rebecca came into his arms.

"Oh, no, Juan, my dear, sweet Juan. It's best that we never go beyond that moment of mutual desire."

"Better? Why?"

Rebecca could feel the urgent pressure of his erect manhood against her lower belly, and her heart raced. It would be . . . so nice. A stolen moment, sweeter for its fleeting nature. Sternly, she rallied her forces.

"Because my dear and valued friend, nothing could come of it except the pleasure of the minute."

A lopsided grin spread on Juan's dark face. "It would take more than a minute, I guarantee you that."

"So it would," Rebecca agreed. "And afterwards . . ." Abruptly she broke from his embrace. "You can't help but know that Ian and I are . . . well, rather close. I could never face him with a guilty secret like that. That's on the one hand. On the other, were I to do what I feel I should and tell him, and it angered him, then I would lose both of you."

She stood for a moment, spread-legged, hands on hips, then sighed gustily and hurried to where he waited. With mounting passion she kissed him. Her tongue traced his lips, attacked his small white teeth, probed deeply into his sweet-tasting mouth, Rebecca moaned and pressed against him. Then with the suddeness with which it had begun, she ended their embrace.

"No. No, no, no, no," Rebecca repeated furiously to herself. She took Juan by one elbow and steered him firmly toward the door. There she stopped him again.

"Get your men on the way. Ian and Hester are

expecting me shortly in the dining room. I must get ready. I . . ."

Juan beamed at her. "That was the most marvelous kiss I've ever had," he said in a little-boy voice. "I'll remember it always."

Then he was gone. Rebecca wanted to throw something, anything, to relieve the enormous head of steam she had built up.

A sentry leaned against the gatepost at Casa Rogelio. He adjusted his posture and held a Winchester repeater across his chest in nearly approved military fashion when Lone Wolf sauntered up on his chestnut gelding.

"Whoa there. What'er you doin' ridin' in here alone?" the guard demanded.

"I got separated from the other boys. We had a long haul and pushed through the night. Somewhere up in them damned mountains, I took a wrong turn, or they did, and we never got together again. I made it back here, so I figure it's them who are lost. What's so important about this Mexican that we all have to be here?"

The hardcase looked thoughtfully at Lone Wolf, then blinked and relaxed slightly. If he knew about the big-shot Mexican coming, he had to be one of them, sure enough.

"Ain't so much for him," he told the strange gunman. "It's because of the forty or so gunhands he's bringing' along."

Lone Wolf's eyebrows rose. "That's one hell of a lot of Mexicans, you ask me."

"Don't you just know it. I get an itchy spot between my shoulderblades thinkin' about that many greasers all in one place. Ride on in. It's past noonin', but the cook can fix you up with somethin'."

"Obliged."

He'd made it. So far, at least, Lone Wolf amended as he walked his mount to the corral, dismounted and followed his nose to the cookshed. He hadn't eaten in twenty-four hours and the lack began to strain. Heady aromas from inside the squat structure brought a generous flow of saliva to his mouth.

"Feller at the gate said I could get something to eat here," he told the apron-wearing Mexican at the big cookstove.

"*Sí.* I feex chu a plate."

The cook produced a large tin plate, heaped it with beans, some coarse-grained meat in a pungent gravy, and a heap of hot corn tortillas. Lone Wolf's stomach cramped at the delightful odors. He thanked the master of the kitchen and walked to an empty trestle table beyond a thin partition.

Lone Wolf was mopping at the last of the juices on his plate when a commotion rose outside in the area between the outer wall and the main house. Some fifteen men rode up, he noted, all Mexicans, shouting and cavorting their horses in a show of high spirit. Voices rose in greeting, and, curious, Lone Wolf returned his utensils and strolled out for a look.

He covered some thirty feet of hard-packed ground when from ahead of him a voice crackled with command. "You! Come closer to me. Keep your hand away from that *pistola*, eh?"

Uncertain, Lone Wolf advanced as directed. He did his best to keep his face obscured. His interrogator would have none of that.

"Look up at me, *gringo. Do it!*"

Reluctantly Lone Wolf raised his head. He saw a vaguely familiar face, now splitting wide with a wolfish grin.

"I thought so, See him, *hombres*? He is one of those

163

who drove us away from that stagecoach we tried to rob down on the desert last week, no? It is the very man. You two," the command came. "Take his gun and hold him tight. He'll not be so lucky this time."

In that instant Lone Wolf recalled the man and had a name for him.

Rudolfo Mateo.

Chapter 18

Even the birds seemed to go silent in the frozen second after Rudolfo Mateo spoke. The two men he had indicated started toward Lone Wolf. The nearer one reached out to grasp him by the left biceps. At that point, the white Crow warrior exploded into furious action.

Whipping his right arm across his body, Lone Wolf grasped the hardcase at the elbow and swung him around, effectively using the startled gunman as a shield between himself and Mateo. With his freed left arm he drew his tomahawk and hurled it at the second would-be captor. It struck solidly and buried to the haft in the screaming victim's chest. A revolver blasted close by and Lone Wolf felt the wind of the bullet's passage. He released his momentary prisoner long enough to draw his six-gun.

Before the human shield could move, Lone Wolf sent a shot over his shoulder from so close that it singed the hair on the right side of his head and permanantly deafened his right ear. The slug went on to crease the leather on the ornate pommel of Mateo's saddle. It caused the *bandido* to duck to one side. When he did, Lone Wolf fired again, this time at another outlaw. A grunt of pain followed a meaty smack and the Mexican bandit slid from his saddle. Men on foot warily closed in.

"Take him alive!" Rudolfo Mateo shouted. "I want him around for questioning."

Their task made no more easier by this injunction, the Anglo and Mexican gunhawks jockeyed for an opening. Not restrained by this command, Lone Wolf downed two more who tried to rush him. They writhed on the ground, blood streaming from minor wounds. Only one round left, he realized. He'd try to make it count. Turning once more, he aimed at Mateo.

The slug went wild when a burly American tackled Lone Wolf from behind. In an instant he went down in a flurry of fists and flying boots. Punches and kicks thudded into the meaty portions of Lone Wolf's body. A few found vulnerable spots. Over the noises of the melee, Rudolfo Mateo's voice sounded crisp and demanding.

"*Basta! Con eso basta, hombres.* Enough," he repeated in English.

Staggered, his head ringing, Lone Wolf was dragged to his feet. Blood seeped from a split lip. The small of his back felt as though a blacksmith had used it for an anvil. Rudolfo Mateo dismounted and walked over to where the bandits held their captive. He pushed his face close to Lone Wolf's.

"Now, *señor*, you are going to tell us a lot of things. Take him to the barn. I will notify Don Rogelio of what has happened."

"That won't be necessary, Don Rudolfo." Roger Styles shouldered his way through the crowd of hardcases. "I heard the disturbance and came to see what might have gone wrong. How delighted I am to see a familiar face." His tone turned raspy with barely concealed hatred. "Well, Baylor. Wherever you are, that bitch Rebecca Caldwell can't be far away. I have some interesting instruments of persuasion which I'm going to enjoy exercising on you to learn her where-abouts. Do as Don Rudolfo ordered," he concluded airily to Lone Wolf's captors.

Fifteen minutes later, Roger entered the barn. He wore black leather trousers and boots, no shirt, and a fanciful black hood of the same material, which covered only part of his face. He looked like someone preparing to enjoy himself immensely. With a brisk, businesslike rubbing of his hands, he stepped over to a rack of torture implements and selected a thumb screw.

"Now then, let's see what we can wring out of you, shall we?"

Roger crossed to where his henchmen had chained Lone Wolf to a wall. He attached the infamous device to Lone Wolf's left thumb and tightened it only enough to insure his victim felt the pressure. A fleeting smile twisted Roger's lips and he licked them with a small crescent of pink tongue. A sigh escaped him, one of an erotic rather than an anticipatory nature.

"I don't suppose it would do any good to ask you straight out where Rebecca Caldwell can be found, now would it?"

"She's in San Diego." Lone Wolf answered simply. Confident of her safety in Ian Claymore's hands and under the protection of Alonzo Horton, he saw no reason to withhold this information.

"My, my, you gave that up easily enough. Couldn't be that you're terrified of being maimed, eh?"

"Fuck off, Roger. You and your scum were run out of San Diego. You aren't about to go back there."

Roger tightened the screw a quarter-turn. Lone Wolf winced, though he remained silent. "Well then, perhaps I should ask what it is she intends to do about me. Are you ready to give that up, too?"

Silence. Lone Wolf affected an insolent smile and braced himself. Roger tightened the screw a half-turn and a thin crimson line appeared around the base of the plunger.

"Another half-turn and it should burst the bone. Not a pleasant sensation, I guarantee you. Answer me. What has Rebecca Caldwell in mind for me?"

"To kill you, of course."

"How and when?"

More silence. Roger tightened the evil instrument. "When will she attack? Where?"

A muffled grinding noise came from Lone Wolf's clenched teeth. Roger reached for the thumb screw. Before he could apply more pressure, Rudolfo Mateo opened the door to the torture chamber and stepped inside.

"Pardon me, Don Rogelio. My *patrón*, Don Pablo Ordaz, has arrived with his men."

"Damn. Right when it was getting interesting." Reluctantly Roger released the torture device. "I'll be back later to continue this fascinating conversation. Meanwhile, do hang around, will you?"

Ian Claymore came to Rebecca Caldwell's room late in the afternoon, his face grave. "Juan's here. There's been some trouble."

"What? What is it? Is . . . Lone Wolf . . . ?"

"Juan wants to tell you himself. He's in the lobby."

Some reticence caused by their last, intimate meeting? Rebecca considered it only fleetingly as she slid a shawl around her creamy rounded shoulders and left the room.

Below, amid the pink Carrera marble columns of the lobby, she met with Juan Lachusa. Seated uncomfortably in a red plush wing chair, he rose to his feet at her approach, his face furrowed with worry lines.

"My men have returned, Miss Rebecca. One of them got in close to the old hacienda on the rancho. He

. . . well, he was there to see our friend, Lone Wolf, captured by the bandits who are gathered there. I'm . . . sorry."

"Was this outside the hacienda?"

"No. Inside the new wall that is being built around the main buildings."

"Then Roger knows all about it. Lone Wolf would never tell him anything, but he's smart enough to make some clever guesses. We've got to do something fast. Ian, Juan, we have to organize some way to break Lone Wolf out of Roger's hands before we are confronted by a disaster."

"Any ideas?"

"Can you obtain the materials you need for those nasty bombs of yours, Ian?"

The minister nodded soberly, reluctantly. "I can, and better, actually. It'll take the rest of today, though. Perhaps longer."

"Then do it at once. Hurry all you can, please."

"This white warrior of the Crow people means a lot to you, Miss Rebecca?"

"Yes, he does, Juan. Much more than is sometimes obvious," she answered without hesitation. "The three warriors who came with you, Juan. Are they willing to fight?"

Lachusa grinned. "Willing? They're right out anxious to fight. We can be ready whenever you say."

"Good. We'll make more plans as we see what we have to fight with. Maybe Sheriff Hunsaker can provide a few more men. I'll go see."

"I would think Jefe Vasquez would be more inclined to render, uh, unofficial assistance," Juan suggested.

"Then I'll call on him at once."

Ten minutes later, a police officer in a blue double-breasted uniform tunic ushered Rebecca into the office of the chief of police. The impeccably dressed silver-haired gentleman with the flowing walrus mustache looked up, eyes atwinkle with sincere welcome. He gestured to a chair.

"Ah, the Señorita Caldwell. I am glad to see you again. Please, sit down and tell me what it is you wish."

"Thank you, Chief Vasquez. Forgive me, but I must be brief. One of my associates, Brett Baylor, has been taken captive by Roger Styles and his gunmen."

Vasquez frowned. "That is serious. Where did this happen? And when?"

"Early this morning, at Rancho Jamul. Not the present ranch handquarters, but the old abandoned hacienda, I'm told."

"Unfortunately, that is out of my jurisdiction. You would have to see Sheriff Hunsaker for any official action."

"I'm aware of that. I'm here at the suggestion of Juan Lachusa, who informed me that you might be inclined to provide . . . ah, *unofficial* assistance. I have another companion, Juan, and three Diegueño warriors to mount a quiet raid on the place and free Lone . . . uh, Brett."

" 'Warriors?' " Vasquez spoke in a bemused, almost patronizing tone. "I wasn't aware there were any Diegueño warriors."

Rebecca hardened her voice. "There are now. Ever since Roger Styles started attacking their villages and murdering people. That's beside the point. My needs now are for some five or so additional guns to insure we can pull this off."

"You're an amazing woman, Señorita Caldwell. But, then, I said that before. These men? Would they necessarily need to be police officers?"

"Oh, no. Not at all, Chief Vasquez. So long as they know how to use a gun and were willing to do so."

"There will be fighting?"

"I don't expect Roger Styles to turn Brett free voluntarily. If we go about it with force, there's bound to be some shooting."

"Nicely put. When would they be needed?"

"Within one hour. I understand the road is in good condition out that far. We rode over much of it on the way here from Julian, so I am familiar with the terrain."

"If perhaps these five men could be located, where should they meet you?"

"Anderson's livery would be fine."

"At two this afternoon? Well then, I wish you luck, señorita."

"That's astonishing, Don Pablo," Roger Styles exclaimed. "You say you ride freely through most of northern Baja California without a single soldier or lawman to resist you?"

"Quite true, Don Rogelio," El Coronel replied blandly.

Pablo Ordaz and the forty *bandidos* riding with him had arrived late, typically so, Roger thought. An entire day, for all it mattered. The introductions, flowery compliments, and several relaxing drinks had been long completed. This meeting of powerful equals had taken the usual Latin turn, with inconsequental conversation for some half-hour. Now the real business could be approached. At least, so Roger thought, when the bandit chieftain, Pablo Ordaz, who styled himself as The Colonel and affected the dress of an army officer, made a passing remark about the scarcity of law officers and military in Baja California, the Mexican state and territory directly south of San Diego County.

"There are not more than four companies of soldiers between Tijuana and Mexicali on the border and

Mulege, halfway down the peninsula. What government workers are present to administer the daily operations of the state or cities are as corrupt as the managers of the mines further south. Slavery has been forbidden in Mexico since eighteen thirty-four. Yet the mine owners and operators of bordellos regularly buy all the people they need to keep in operation. My *segundo*, Rudolfo, has made you aware of this, no?"

"Definitely. A profitable sideline, as I have found. My goal, however, is to become the absolute master of much of Southern California. To make it my own little domain."

"Wouldn't it be nice to add to that all of Baja California? Between us, Don Rogelio, we could become millionaires a hundred times over."

Roger's ambition vaulted to the heavens. Millions of dollars for the taking. It sounded so nice. Could he trust this El Coronel? Of course not. But then, once they had realized their great design, the fat, stupid Mexican could be done away with. That would leave Roger alone, with his hands on all those millions.

"We could take the whole peninsula within a matter of three or four months. The use of ships would help. If we moved with speed, we could even cut that time factor down," Ordaz continued.

"This is the most remarkable scheme I've ever run into," Roger praised. "One I could hardly say no to. Let's begin plans on such an endeavor tomorrow. Tonight there is a small fiesta to celebrate your presence and the joining of our forces. Details can come later, eh?"

"*Sí como no*. My sentiments exactly. Rudolfo tells me a spy has been captured here at your *estancia*. Is there any danger of compromising our plans?"

"None at all. Come. If you like, I'll show you this, ah, spy. He's rather a sorry specimen, actually."

172

In the barn, Lone Wolf hung in his chains, conserving himself for the ordeal he knew would eventually come. When the yellow light of a kerosene lamp brightened the windowless room, he looked up to see Roger Styles and a thick-waisted Mexican in a military uniform. What could this be about?"

"I see you're awake, Baylor. This is El Coronel, a famous and powerful *bandido* in Mexico. He is here to join me in my conquest of California. Then we are going on to take the Mexican state of Baja California. So, you see, you lump of filth, you are in the presence of persons of considerable importance. Perhaps that will loosen your tongue."

Lone Wolf gathered what he could of his scant saliva and spat fully in Roger's face. Roger recoiled as though punched in the mouth. El Coronel stepped forward and backhanded the trussed prisoner. Then he slashed across Lone Wolf's face with a riding crop. Roger held out a restraining hand.

"Your pardon, please, Don Pablo. There's no science in such techniques. Here, let me give you an example of the finer arts of interrogation." Roger walked to the table of instruments and selected one. He held it gleaming in the light, turning it so the facets reflected off his victim's face.

"Ah, yes, this should do nicely. You know, I often wondered," he confided to the bandit chief, "if perhaps some of my ancestors weren't members of the Santa Hermandad."

Mention of the infamous Spanish Inquisition made even Pablo Ordaz shudder.

Chapter 19

Their small posse had left San Diego at two-thirty in the afternoon. Hard riding had brought them to the large, fruitful valley that contained the main portion of Rancho Jamul by sunset. They rode through a low pass, formed by enfolding hills, and followed the lead of one of the Dieguéño warriors who had located Roger Styles's headquarters. By eight-thirty Rebecca and Ian, along with Juan and his Diegueños and the five off-duty policemen, reached a point where they could see the bright lights of large bonfires and hear the wild abandon of mariachi music.

"That's "Sonora Querida" they're playing," Juan whispered. With all that noise there was no need for speaking softly. The young man had been caught up in the excitement of their impromptu raid.

"Let's hope they keep the party going long enough for us to find Lone Wolf and release him," Rebecca responded tightly.

"The problem is going to be in getting back out," Ian opined.

"That's what your delightful little devices are for," Rebecca reminded him.

The sandy-haired, long-faced Scot produced a dour

expression. "Where do you want me to put them?"

"A couple along the road into the place, of course, facing the hacienda. When we pick a spot along the wall to go in and out, the rest can be set up to cover that area. Anyone chasing us over it, or firing from behind it, will get a nasty surprise."

Ian grimaced. "I can't be everywhere at once. The policemen I've instructed know what to do. I think the best idea is for me to come with you."

For a moment, Rebecca considered this, then gave him a soft pat on the hand. "There should be at least three of us. Juan's going; you might as well, too. Given another hour or two of this and the men in there will be drunk enough they'll have a hard time seeing straight. That's when we'll move in."

"This is some fiesta, Don Rogelio," El Coronel complimented his host.

Roger Styles beamed. "Thank you, Don Pablo. Tomorrow morning our bargain will be sealed and then you'll see a real celebration."

"How's that? There's two whole beeves on the spits, rice, beans, fresh shellfish, everything one could ask for, Don Rogelio."

"I talked with that funny little fellow whom Don Rudolfo identified as your personal cook. We'll have *carnitas* with all the trimmings, *pollos asado* and *cabrito*. Your favorites, I was given to understand. The *vaqueros* among your men have offered to provide us with a *Chariada*. Then, the highlight of the day will be the execution of Brett Baylor. Once Lone Wolf, uh, Baylor, is out of the way, it'll be that much easier to get rid of Rebecca Caldwell."

Sensitive to Roger's mood, Pablo Ordaz pursed his lips a moment in silent speculation, accepted another full, foaming mug of beer from a servant, and decided.

He might find the information to be of value when the time came to dispose of this dullard *gringo* and become "Emperor of California" himself. Until then, he would do all he could to please his new partner.

"This woman, Rebecca Caldwell. Tell me about her, please."

"It isn't a flattering story, Don Pablo," Roger admitted with a frown. "She is obsessed with hunting me down for wrongs against her and her mother that she believes me responsible for."

"And were you?"

"Not directly. I'm sure you never heard of Bitter Creek Jake Tulley. He had a gang that operated for my benefit. At one time Jake and his boys had to make an exchange to keep from being killed off by the Sioux. Rebecca was part of that trade. When she managed to get away from the Oglala camp where she'd lived for five years, she started out to get vengeance against Tulley and his men. During the course of this she found out my connection to the gang and has been after me ever since. More than seven times now she has managed to show up in an area where I had invested a great deal and destroyed all my efforts. She's not beaten me, only depleted my resources. The man we were questioning this afternoon has been her companion from the start. What it means is that she's close at hand. Once I've eliminated her, there will be no bar to my success. Why, between us, you and I can carve out a sizable empire in this raw and unsettled land."

"Mexico would do little about the loss of Baja California. And what they did do would be done badly. But what of *los estados unidos*? What would your country do when we, ah, seize some of the land it claims?"

"There's more here than the United States will ever need or use. Once we establish lawful ownership over much of it, and institute our rule, other countries will recognize us as a soverign nation. Then they'll not dare anything. 'Manifest Destiny' is playing itself out well north of us. Although quick to anger and to defend their individual rights and property, the majority of Americans believe that bullshit the government puts out about not having any imperalistic designs. There would be a loud clammor to not have the government take action.

"In a way, you have it better in Mexico. There the, ah, masses don't have all that much say over those in power, although you have adopted the trappings of a republic. The same sort of system will work for us. And we'll be rich, my friend!"

Before Pablo Ordaz could reply, a roughly dressed gunman hurried to Roger's side. "Sorry to disturb your conversation," he began politely. "There's reports of someone prowlin' around outside the wall."

"How many?"

"Not sure, Mr. Styles. Could be half a dozen or a whole army."

"Has anyone seen them clearly?"

"No, sir. It's dark and all these bright lights in here make it hard to see beyond what's lit up."

"Send some men out to look it over."

"I've already done so. Mr. Walsh told me the same thing."

"Good," Roger responded in dismissal. Then to his guest, "I've great trust in Dooley Walsh. You haven't met him, have you, Don Pablo? Come over and we'll make you acquainted now."

Roger had taken only a single step when a shot blasted into the night from the direction of the barn. Nearly dropping his glass, Roger turned in that direction, mouth agape.

Bruised and bleeding, his skin blistered and reddened in places from burns, Lone Wolf lay in a heap on the floor of the torture chamber. His chains had been fastened to rings near the base of the wall, so that he had no hope of escape. Despite the fog of shock and pain-induced exhaustion, he could dimly hear the noise of the festivities on the far side of the compound. Total darkness surrounded him and his ears strained to hear the least sound. Vague impressions of the long tormenting by Roger Styles warned him he would have to rally his waning strength in the event of another session. Not until the door creaked open, bringing with it a shaft of pale yellow light, did he become aware of the furtive activity close at hand.

"This has to be it," a voice well familiar to him whispered. Rebecca!

"Let's be quick about it," Ian Claymore's baritone rumble replied.

They entered, dark silhouettes against the outer brightness. Lone Wolf tried to raise himself and speak. His words came out a pitiful croak.

"Over there," Rebecca declared at once.

Then she knelt at his side. Her hand felt cool on his fevered cheek. Ian Claymore arrived with a welcome canteen. He'd not eaten nor had a restoring drink since his capture. Eagerly Lone Wolf swallowed the marvelous liquid.

"He's chained to the wall," Ian announced.

"We'll have to get them off somehow, only . . . we can't make any noise."

"Kaw-ke-keys over there," Lone Wolf forced out. Ian rose and swiftly crossed the room.

"By the spirits, what have they done to you?" Rebecca blurted.

"La'er. Ge-t me loose."

Ian returned with a thick iron ring, which contained half a dozen keys. "It'll only take a minute, my friend," he reassured the captive.

The fourth key did it. Freed of his restraint, Lone Wolf attempted to stand, only to totter and fall against Rebecca's shoulder, a groan of agony ripped from his throat.

"Burnt my . . . my feet."

"Can you walk at all? We can't carry you."

"Moccasins," Lone Wolf suggested. "An' . . . my . . . my horse . . ."

"We'll come back for him. This isn't our last visit to Roger Styles."

A limp bundle in one corner turned out to be Lone Wolf's clothing. He dressed with Ian's help and slid his feet into moccasins. He winced, unseen in the darkness, and gingerly applied pressure. Cushioned now, the blisters on the soles of his feet did not send out the violent pain signals of a minute ago. With assistance, he walked unsteadily to the doorway.

There he had to rest. Within five minutes the trio had reached the rear entrance to the barn. Beyond it lay darkness. Behind them, in the center and far edges of the compound, wild music came from guitars, trumpets, and small wooden Veracruz harps. Men shouted and sang, laughed and roved about. Rebecca held her breath, fearful lest some of them come to the barn for some purpose. When Lone Wolf indicated he felt ready to continue, they left for the wall. Rebecca experienced considerable relief.

Only to be shattered a moment later when a voice challenged them from the darkness. "You there! Who are you and where do you think you're going?"

"It's me an' Charlie," Ian replied with quickwitted acumen. "He's taken on too much to drink. Thought I'd let him puke it out over the wall."

"Good thinkin'. C'mon then." Then, a moment later when the trio drew nearer. "Say, I don't know you.

What's that woman . . . ?"

Ian's long, powerful leg flashed out and the toe of his boot caught the suspicious sentry full in the crotch. Air wheezed out of him and he staggered backward a step before abruptly sitting on the ground. Involuntary tears squeezed from his tightly closed eyelids. In a rush, Ian closed in and smashed the barrel of his Remington down on the man's head. He turned and motioned to Rebecca.

Quickly she brought Lone Wolf to the wall. Together they boosted him up onto the lip. Rebecca followed, and then Ian. Juan Lachusa joined them from the darkness.

"There was another guard about fifty feet away. I took care of him with my knife," he informed the others.

"Let's make tracks," Ian suggested.

They had covered half the distance to where the deadly explosive charges waited when a voice challenged them from behind. "Who's out there? Hold up, damnit!"

A shot erupted in the night, revealing an orange-red muzzle bloom a ways down the wall. "I thought you'd taken care of the sentry," Rebecca chided Juan.

"I did. One in the other direction."

"This other one's going to have company real soon," Ian suggested. "We have to hurry for sure."

More muzzle flashes followed the first. Rebecca glanced back to count seven gunmen firing blindly into the night. Dark figures topped the wall and dropped to the ground. Pursuit had already begun. Only twenty yards remained to safety. She started to run.

Ian and Juan, half-dragging Lone Wolf, reached her beside the first prepared charge. Ian knelt, struck a lucifer match, and ignited the fuse. Swiftly they scrambled into the concealing brush. Running footsteps sounded near. Then the night turned bright white.

So close to the source, the blast could barely be distinguished from the force of the ground and air shock waves. The crouching figures jolted and swayed. Beyond the spot where the terrible bomb went off, they clearly distinguished the screams of the wounded and dying.

From the wall an awed voice questioned, "What the hell was that?"

"I don't know, but we've gotta go out there and finish the job," another man commanded.

Rebecca and Ian moved instantly to the next pair of murderous charges. They waited, making certain that men rushed in their direction from the wall, before lighting the frayed ends of dynamite fuse.

When the dual bombs went off, seven more men gave their lives for Roger's vainglorious scheme.

"Christ!" a hardcase exclaimed. "We're bein' attacked by some sort of army. Send a couple dozen men on horseback to get behind them."

A short while later, the clatter of horses' hooves sounded from inside the compound. They grew louder, then cut off in the ear-scouring twin blasts of the mines covering the road. At the strident urging of a bass voice, more men went over the wall in two places. Again, Rebecca and Ian set off the powerful charges.

For a moment, daylight brightness illuminated both of them. In its fading glow, rifles crackled from the compound and bullets cracked through the air, entirely too close. Rebecca and Ian dropped to the ground.

"It's time to pull out," Rebecca suggested. "You and Juan take care of Lone Wolf, I'll go get the others."

"Be careful," Ian cautioned.

Another blast fractured the air. Long, rolling bellows echoed along the steep canyon walls. As the light faded, Rebecca snaked away, intent on rounding up their small force and withdrawing without casualties. One thing for certain, Roger would know she'd been there.

"That woman," Pablo Ordaz snapped. "Did you see her? The one out there behind those infernal explosions. She's the one who fought against some of my men when they tried to rob a stage."

" 'That woman,' as you put it, Don Pablo, is Rebecca Caldwell," Roger informed him gloomily.

Chapter 20

Blackness surrounded Rebecca Caldwell and her small force as they raced away from the rancho. The moonless night provided an advantage, yet could turn into a hazard without warning. They had covered half a mile when the last two bombs detonated.

Ian had left them behind, rigged with friction fuse ignitors and a trip-wire. It served as a good gauge of how far behind any pursuit might be. Without need for discussion, the pace increased. If the blast created enough confusion they had a chance. If it didn't, they might all die in the savory-smelling chapparal. After ten minutes at a brisk canter, Rebecca signaled for a halt.

In the quiet of the night ears strained for any sound of hoofbeats. Rebecca could hear none, and a moment later Lone Wolf confirmed her conclusion.

"If they're still after us, they're walking," he remarked confidently. "Those last two bombs must have given them a nasty surprise."

"Some of them saw us standing nearby when the first ones went off," Ian said slowly. "If any who did went along, they'll naturally think some of us are still around the hacienda. That would have to be checked out before they went on."

"Also," Rebecca added, a trace of relief in her voice, "after that last explosion, they would have to move slowly to make sure there were no more waiting for them. That's the way it worked up in that canyon against the Hollisites."

Her explanation had been for the benefit of the police officers, who showed signs of discomfort and worry. The five men sat close to Rebecca, listening carefully to the conversation.

"It'll be daylight before we get back to San Diego," Juan Lachusa offered.

"That can't come soon enough for me," Rebecca responded.

Chaos.

Roger Styles could think of no other way to describe the incredible, firelit scene at his Casa Rogelio. Men swarmed around in confusion, some firing into the darkness at unknown targets. Half of the riders who had gone after that damned Rebecca Caldwell and her henchmen had been wiped out by more of those infernal explosive devices. It seemed impossible to him that any of them would have remained behind to set them off. It would be too much of a risk.

Dooley Walsh hurried up to Roger, his face streaked with power grime. "We must have lost fifteen men, Roger. And Rudolfo says at least that many of El Coronel's *bandidos* got it. How the hell could something like that happen?"

"Rebecca Caldwell," Roger snarled, the name sounding like something unclean that had crawled out of an outhouse pit. "We got careless and she took advantage of it, damn her."

"But . . . but to use artillery?"

"Not cannon, Dooley. Some sort of bombshell, like a

mortar uses. I . . . don't know for sure. We'll learn more after daylight. Maybe they left some behind. Whatever the case, I want that woman found and eliminated. Get some men ready to leave for San Diego at daylight. That's where she has to have come from and where she'll return. Now, I want to talk to Ordaz."

Roger found the potbellied bandit chieftain talking excitedly with a group of his followers. Ordaz excused himself and walked agitatedly over to Roger.

"For one who commands so many men, Señor Styles, it seems remarkable that you are unable to defeat a mere woman. Perhaps it would not be wise for our alliance to be concluded?"

Despite his flare of anger at the slur, a finger of panic touched Roger's spine. "Oh, no, no, Don Pablo, uh . . . El Coronel. You must understand, especially after what has happened, that Rebecca Caldwell is no 'mere woman,' as you put it. She's . . . she's like Nemisis."

"Who?"

"In Greek mythology," Roger patiently explained, "there is a goddess of retribution, named Nemisis. Once sentence has been passed on a mortal by Zeus, she cannot be swayed from her course. She stalks her victim until justice, as seen by the other gods and goddesses, is done."

"A fanciful story to frighten children," Ordaz dismissed. He gave Roger a shrewd look. "And perhaps a heresy, as *la eglácia* would have it. But we are men and not to be frightened by such nonsense, no? We must find this woman and kill her. It is bad for, uh, morale."

"I've already made arrangements to send men to where she'll feel safest, find her, and finish her off."

"Good. Perhaps then, after this deed is done, we can still talk business."

A soft, salt-tanged breeze rippled the waves on San

Diego bay. After a brief rest and a hurried breakfast, Rebecca and her companions met with Alonzo Horton and Chief Vasquez. Rebecca made a careful report of what had happened and what they had observed. Lone Wolf gave details of the grandiose plans he had heard discussed by Roger and the bandit chief Roger called Don Pablo. To say the least, the information created a sensation. It also failed to pleased San Diego's premier entrepreneur.

"That's a damning report," Horton said forcefully. "Unfortunately, it is still nothing that can be used in court. It would be their word against yours. How many of this outlaw army do you feel were, ah, incapacitated?"

"No way of telling," Rebecca replied. "Quite a few, I would guess. Ian's explosives take quite a toll."

"Your earlier mention of these devices caught my attention. What are they?"

Ian flushed slightly. "The bombs are quite simple, really. I've refined them somewhat over the first ones. The ones we used last night consisted of a thick iron plate, with a lip extending around the outer edge. I filled the inner surface with dynamite and bits of iron, some pistol balls, and the like. Then a thick paper disc is secured over the top with wax. When the bomb is set off, the iron plate provides just enough resistance so that the majority of the explosive force is projected outward, taking the shrapnel with it."

Alonzo Horton blanched and he grimaced before replying. "A grisly-sounding instrument, to say the least. How effective are they?"

"For anyone directly in front of one, up to twenty-five feet away, one-hundred-percent kill."

"My God. I certainly hope the military never learns of these things. Mr. Baylor," Horton went on to change from the unpalatable subject. "In what you overheard, did you gain any idea of their future plans?"

"Only sketchily," Lone Wolf responded. "They talked about driving all the Indians out of San Diego County, killing them if necessary, and taking the land. Also about seizing Baja California, whatever that is."

"The Mexican territory, a peninsula, to the immediate south of us," Horton answered absently. His mind churned with the implications of this information. "My word, this man Styles knows no bounds to his ambition. I'm not so certain, given enough men and equipment, he couldn't carry off such a scheme. I must talk with Sheriff Hunsaker, see about mounting some sizable force to launch against Styles. Will you join your efforts with ours?"

Tempting though the offer was, Rebecca had other plans. "I'm sorry to say we won't, Alonzo. There are a lot of Indians who deserve to get justice for their losses. We've decided to throw our lot in with them."

"But that . . ." Horton blurted. He grasped the arms of his chair and gathered his clamoring thoughts. "I'm not entirely certain that would be legal."

"Legal or not, it's a certain way to insure there will be no trouble from the Cahuilla and the Diegueños among law-abiding citizens. If they can fight their real enemy, they'll be satisfied."

Horton pondered her words a moment. "Hmmm. I suppose you have a point there. Naturally, nothing, uh, official can be involved with such an enterprise."

"We understand. I wish you luck," Rebecca responded, rising. "We're leaving for Baron Long immediately after our noon meal."

A full day of work restored nearly all of the damage done in the raid on Casa Rogelio. When a saucy rooster signaled the beginning of another day, laborers from among the squatters on the old rancho gathered to complete the task. Still furious, Roger stalked about the small fortress snapping out orders and urging more speed. He had no idea what might happen next. Pablo Ordaz and half of his men rode out to raid some Indian villages, leaving the *estancia* severely undermanned. Shortly before noon, the men sent on the previous day to San Diego returned.

"They're gone," the leader reported to Roger.

"What do you mean by that?"

"They left San Diego yesterday afternoon."

"Headed here?" Icy apprehension touched Roger and released an involuntary shudder.

"No. Took a long time to find out, but I got it from a feller who works at the livery. They headed for Barona . . . the Indian reservation."

"Where's that?"

"North and east of us about thirty-five miles."

"Damn! A day's journey. What could they be going there for?" Roger speculated aloud.

"It's for certain it's not anything we'll like," Dooley Walsh offered. His cold, blue-gray stare made Roger uncomfortable.

"The thing is, what can we do about it?"

"Wait and see, I'd say."

"Not with Rebecca Caldwell involved, Dooley. Waiting for her to come to us could invite sure disaster. We ought . . . we ought to send a strong force there to attack, catch the Indians and Rebecca off guard. Or perhaps set up an ambush and trap her in the open."

"Good idea, Roger," Dooley agreed.

"It makes more sense than waiting," Rudolfo Mateo offered in support of Roger's plan. "Half of the men left under my command will be at your disposal, Don Rogelio."

"Thank you, Don Rudolfo. I appreciate that. My only worry is, will that leave enough here to protect the hacienda?"

"It should be plenty," Dooley assured him. "I doubt she'll be able to organize any sort of second attack so soon."

Roger smiled for the first time since the gunshot near the barn had heralded the surprise raid. "We'll do it then. Get the men ready, Don Rudolfo. You'll command the expedition."

Chapter 21

A sky painfully blue and utterly cloudless formed an unfathomable dome over the emerald fields of Baron Long. Naked children shouted shrilly and cavorted at the sides of the horses. An entirely different sort of reception greeted Rebecca Caldwell and her companions this time. Juan Lachusa had sent ahead two of the young Diegueño men to relay the information regarding their results. In response, a group of young women of marriageable age gathered to sing in beautiful voices. They waved fronds of palmetto cactus and swayed from side to side as they expressed a ritual welcome. The young men hurried toward the council field, shouting excitedly. Several oldsters fired off ancient muzzle loading rifles in celebration.

"You'd think we had already won the war," Rebecca remarked in an aside to Lone Wolf.

"Finding out what we have learned so far is sure to have relieved a lot of worried minds," he replied. "The thing to discover now is whether they'll fight an organized force like Roger's."

In spite of his injuries, Lone Wolf had insisted on accompanying the raiders to the Diegueño village. Even after medical attention by Alonzo Horton's personal physician he ached all over, and several of the lacerations had turned dark red, indicating infection. Regardless, he had every intention of being in on the final assault against Roger Styles. Roger owed him, Lone Wolf believed.

"They will," Juan answered quickly. "You can be sure of that. Ewi will see to it. The chiefs made an agreement and they'll carry it out."

Ewi met them with open arms, a wide smile spread so that it revealed his nearly toothless condition. "You are welcome among our people," he declared formally. Then, with less attention to custom, he gestured to where the council had gathered. "Come, sit with us and tell us everything."

When the tale had been completed, through Juan's translation, heads nodded enthusiastically around the circle. Rebecca concluded with a question.

"Will the Diegueño join in this one big battle to exterminate your enemy?"

Joyful shouts assaulted her eardrums.

"When do we ride to the place of this man, Styles?" Ewi asked when the excitement quieted.

"Right away," Rebecca answered, anxious to be at it. "We can leave at once, if you wish."

"It is good. First, we want to feast you, show our gratitude. You'll not refuse that, will you?"

"Certainly not," Rebecca told the old chief with a grin. She rubbed her flat stomach. "I, for one, am ready to eat a great deal."

Rudolfo Mateo led twenty-seven men along the only trail between Rancho Jamul and the Diegueño reservation at Barona. They had covered plenty of ground so far and his punitive force showed no sign of tiring. Although Pablo and Don Rogelio believed an ambush to be the best way of eliminating their enemy, he personally preferred the idea of striking at the reservation. In his experience, he'd never found an Indian all that ready to protect a *gringo*, or a Mejicano, for that matter. He might be able, Rudolfo considered, to ride in and claim to be the law. Tell the *indios* he had come to arrest some white criminals. This *gringa* Caldwell would find out then how little help she could expect from the Diegueños.

"The trail grows steeper beyond here, Mateo," one of the riders Rudolfo had sent forward to scout reported. "Also, I am worried. Flores has not returned."

"Should he have?" Rudolfo inquired indifferently.

"*Sí.* We alternate and never ride more than twenty minutes ahead of the main body. He didn't come back in time so I could report to you."

"So, so. Maybe he stopped to water his horse. In any event, we will find out eventually."

Twenty minutes later they did just that. Flores's body lay sprawled in the center of the trail. His horse cropped lush grass a short distance away. Rudolfo signaled for a halt. Before he could shout any orders, two dozen rifles and shotguns opened up from among the rocks and trees. Bullets cracked through the air and swishing columns of buckshot slashed into horseflesh and men alike. Screams of agony echoed from the hillsides.

"Ambush!" Rudolfo shouted. "Ride through, hurry, ride!"

Only they couldn't.

A solid phalynx of thorny brush blocked the trail around the next bend. Arrows moaned their ghostly messages of mayhem and death in a dark cloud. Rattled by this unexpected turn, the bandits wheeled in confusion. Once again Mateo bellowed commands. This time to retreat.

By the time they reached the spot where Flores's corpse lay, another dense picket had been put into place to cut off their escape. Those who had overcome their initial surprise began to return fire. A white flash blinded them a moment before an unbearable noise assailed their eardrums.

Bits of metal slashed into the ranks, felling men and animals. Shrieks and wails came unceasingly from the wounded and dying. Everywhere could be seen the yellow-orange flash of weapons firing, and a thick haze of powder smoke began to obscure all vision. More feathered shafts rained down.

"Down!" Rudolfo commanded. "Use your horses for cover. Aim your shots."

His own mount gave a mighty groan and sagged to its knees. Rudolfo kicked free of the stirrups and managed to avoid being pinned beneath the weight. Cursing mightily in Spanish, he swung his head from side to side in an attempt to locate the enemy. Two bullets slapped horseflesh close enough to his head that blood and shreds of meat spattered his face. Rudolfo ducked low and tried to remember how to pray.

Rebecca Caldwell watched the ambush sprung with surprising efficiency. From her vantage point behind a cluster of large gray boulders, she could make out the identity of several of the outlaws. Too bad Lone Wolf hadn't been able to be here, she thought. He had needed immediate medical care, which the shaman of Baron Long and his assistants provided. Given a few hours to recover his strength, he would come along with the second contingent of warriors, summoned from other villages.

"Get ready to put the other barricade in place," she instructed Juan Lachusa. "They're going to make a run up the trail."

At Juan's signal a picked group of Diegueño men dragged heavy manzanita bushes and thorny chunks of cactus in place across the trail. Then they took their places. Good shots all, they made ready to repel any attempt by the bandits to get past the obstruction and flee toward Roger's stronghold. Rebecca smiled in grim satisfaction. Thirty less gunmen when they got through here. Then they would be ready to take on what force remained at the rancho. A rattling crack of gunfire up the trail swelled to a regular fusillade.

Good. With any kind of leadership at all, the bandits would soon be heading back. Rebecca cocked one of her Smith Americans and made ready to welcome them.

El Coronel received Roger's message with ill grace. The idea of that *gringo cabrón* giving him orders. Then again, he had men for whom he was responsible at the rancho. If another attack came it could go badly for them. He had probably better pull back as Don Rogelio wanted.

"Lupe, Manuel," Pablo Ordaz called out. "Call in the scouts. We are returning to the rancho."

Mierda! How could such a calamity happen? Never before, even when chased by the army in Mexico, had he and his men gotten into such a bad position. Because of one woman? Impossible. Unthinking, he spoke his thoughts aloud.

"Hermano," Pablo addressed his younger brother. "Do you believe that all this is the doing of a single woman? A *gringa* at that?"

"No, Pablo. Such a thing is not possible. This new partner of yours is an incompetent. *Es un persona de influencia de nada.*"

Pablo barked a short laugh. "Well put. A big shot at nothing. I've been thinking the same thing. So, I shall return with half of the men with us. You shall keep the others in, how do they say it in the army? Ah! Reserve. Yes, it would be well to have a force outside that place, in case it is attacked again. You, Jaime, will have the honor of commanding that reserve."

"*Gracias, hermano*. You'll help me pick the men for this force?"

"Certainly."

Could there be only eleven of them left? The realization chilled Rudolfo Mateo. So quickly they had been cut down. What chance had he, or any of them, to escape?

None, the frightening answer echoed in his head.

Should he surrender? If so, to whom? If there were soldiers or lawmen among the Indians, it would mean the gallows. If not, an even worse fate awaited him. Despite his oft-proven courage, Rudolfo shuddered. To be tortured by Indians! *Madre de Dios!*

"Beltran!" he shouted to one of the bandits. *"Tien cuidado!"*

With the reduced numbers, the Indians had become braver. In groups of four and five, they readily exposed themselves, to rush down the sloping hillsides and attack isolated men sheltered behind their dead horses. Such a party now ran toward Guillermo Beltran. Heedless of his own safety, Rudolfo came to the kneeling position and opened fire with his Winchester.

Four fast rounds levered through the action of the model '73. It proved sufficient to scatter the attacking Diegueños, leaving one behind to kick out his life on the blood-splattered grass. Rudolfo breathed a sigh of relief. If they still ran from firepower, he and those left might have a chance. The soft clop of hooves and a whicker came from behind him. If one of their horses had survived, his chances looked even better. Filled with eagerness and hope, Rudolfo Mateo turned to grasp his prize.

Only to look into the big black hole in the muzzle of a Smith and Wesson .44 American. His mouth gaped open. Slowly he raised his eyes to take in the slight, lovely form of the young woman who held the deadly firearm. *It was she!* Rudolfo tried hard to swallow in the second before he fought to bring his Winchester up into line with her proudly pointed breasts.

"Adios, pendejo," Rebecca Caldwell told him softly, a moment before she blasted Rudolfo Mateo into eternity.

"We'll not reach the rancho before the middle of the night," Rebecca told the Diegueño leaders half an hour and a mile down the trail from the ambush site. "So we plan for a sunrise attack. They'll be most vulnerable then."

Nods of agreement went around the cluster. This woman warrior had shown her courage and wisdom more than once. It was not so bad a thing to fight at her side. At a signal from Juan Lachusa everyone remounted and started off toward the distant ranch. Ian Claymore rode at Rebecca's side.

"I wonder what Alonzo Horton and the sheriff managed to come up with?" he speculated aloud.

"We'll see in time," Rebecca answered. "I only hope he brings whatever he arranged to the ranch before we attack. There are too few guns among the Diegueños. Only with thirty men, Roger could hold us off for a long while."

"I have plenty of explosives left. If he meant it about those cannons . . ."

"That would be more than enough to even the odds," Rebecca agreed, cheered somewhat.

"If we can only keep the Diegueños under control,

196

not have them going off after individual glory. Disciplined fire is the answer."

"I watched them back at the ambush. People are right. They don't really know how to fight. At least typical Indian style. They're looking to us for guidance, and so long as we give them good advice, they should do well."

"I'd like to share your confidence. Only it keeps coming to my mind that unseasoned troops also tend to panic and go into a retreat if they meet superior firepower. Their lack of a combative spirit can be a two-edged sword for us. How far behind us should the rest of the Diegueños and the Cahuillas be?"

"They were to have left Baron Long two hours ago. That should put them in position to strike the hacienda from a different direction about half an hour after we open fire."

"Provided nothing goes wrong."

"Ian, in battle you're going to find that something *always* goes wrong."

Chapter 22

She's out there somewhere, plotting, scheming for our down-fall.

The thought swirled through the mind of Roger Styles like the lumps in a thick, meat-scented broth that bubbled in a huge iron kettle over the fire. Roger's personal cook tended to the stew, somewhat put out that the early nighttime mountain chill had driven his master inside at such a critical moment. Jealous of the secret ingredients used to make sensational surprises of each of his dishes, the petulant would-be chef pursed his lips and glowered at Roger's back.

"*Patrón,*" Uvaldo, the major domo called from the doorway. "El Coronel and his men are arriving. Will you greet them outside?"

"No. Send the men to eat and find quarters. Have Don Pablo and his under-officers join me in the dining room. Have Ramon open the bar there."

"*Sí, patrón.* I will do it immediately."

"François," Roger snapped at the cook. "There will be guests for dinner. Prepare a couple of suitable side dishes to go with that stew."

"*Oui, M'iseu.*" Boeuf Bergundia au Champignons could hardly be called a stew. He sniffed angrily behind Roger's departing back.

Roger reached the dining room ahead of the others. He looked about the open, high-ceilinged room, satisfied with what he saw. The herringbone pattern of ocotillo branch vigas had been dusted and de-cobwebbed, and below them, the solid exposed beams glowed with a patina of smoke and age. Shutters had been closed over the outer windows and a fire laid in the dome-shaped fireplace. Roger crossed and touched a match to the dry tinder, then turned as Pablo Ordaz and six bandits entered.

"Don Pablo, you made good time. We should have sufficient forces now."

"Why did you ask me to come back?"

His expression bland, Roger explained that he had learned that Rebecca Caldwell had left San Diego for the Diegueño reservation of Barona. "So, I dispatched your capable captain, Rudolfo Mateo, with a medium force to attack her before anything effective could be brought against us here."

"You should have sent us there also. We could have struck from the east of them and made certain of victory," El Coronel protested.

"True enough," Roger dismissed. "Only I got to thinking that after all Rebecca Caldwell is a devious bitch. She could have put it out that their goal was the reservation as a form of diversion. She would, in fact, be headed here right now with enough men to wipe us out, assuming we had done as we did and divided our strength."

"Hmm. You have a point. And word from Rudolfo?"

"None so far. I don't expect any until some time tomorrow. Come, let's have a drink. Dinner will be ready in a short while."

Roger's heightened spirits continued into the late hours. Tired from a lot of useless riding, as they saw it, Pablo Ordaz and his officers retired around midnight. Roger went to his quarters where, with whip and chains, he entertained another young girl until she bled from many injuries and he found blissful release in her pain-driven shudders.

Mourning doves cooed their doleful salutations as a thin band of pink-tinged white lined the sawtooth ridges to the east. Sixty Diegueño warriors crouched in the dew-moist chaparral surrounding Casa Rogelio. From a spot overlooking the hacienda, Rebecca Caldwell studied the serene vista below.

"If we had some way of driving off those horses, we'd have a big advantage," she observed to Ian Claymore.

"Just so. Only how, without killing them needlessly?"

"That's the problem that's bothered me so far. Could you do something with explosives to blow a hole in that wall, over at the corral?"

Ian frowned. "Those adobe blocks are eighteen inches wide. There's two rows of them with tamped earth between. The wall is eight foot high at that point. That means . . ." He grew silent in rapid calculations. "It would take more dynamite than I have with me. And we'd need time to tunnel underneath and set charges. Give me a week and it could be done."

"Not the best way of going at things. If we could somehow get at the gate on the inside . . . ?"

A grin spread on Ian's wide freckled face. "I thought of that earlier, or at least of the advantage of having someone inside the compound with explosives. Two of Juan's Diegueños have worked as powder men in the mines near Julian. I sent them off with six sticks each about an hour ago. What we need is some way of communicating what we want done."

"I have just the thing. Can you draw a series of small pictures, illustrating where you want charges placed?"

"Sure. But what good . . . ?"

"You make the pictures. Then we can wrap the slip of paper around the shaft of an arrow and shoot it in to where one of the men can get it."

"Provided I can locate one."

"You can with those field glasses you have. Surely you gave them some idea of how best to disrupt the defenders?"

"Yes. There should be one warrior at the back of the barn."

Twenty minutes later the message had been prepared. Although the sky had lightened considerably, dark shadows still bathed the hill-ringed cup that housed the compound of Casa Rogelio. Ian spotted the hiding Dieguéño and pointed out the location to a thick-shouldered archer.

"You'll only have one chance," Ian cautioned the marksman through Juan's interpretation.

Nodding, the man drew back his bowstring and let fly.

An eerie moan wavered in the air as the shaft sped along a high arc and descended into shadow behind the barn. Several seconds passed in tense expectation, then the watchers discerned furtive movement.

Wearing the sombrero, vest, and crossed bandoliers of a *bandido*, the Dieguéño warrior appeared at the front of the barn. He walked in a casual, though direct, manner to the corral gate. There he paused, turned and appeared to gaze inward at the horses. After a while, he squatted and rolled a cigarette. This he stuck in his mouth while he seemed to search for a small stone, suitable for striking a match. Meanwhile, his other hand fumbled at the base of the post. His rock located, he ignited his match, lighted the cigarette and stood erect.

Another short pause and he walked quickly away. Behind him two tendrils of white smoke rose into the cool morning air. A smile of satisfaction spread on Rebecca Caldwell's face. The opening shot in their new campaign would be a loud one.

Roger Styles dreamed of flesh. Tender, silky, female flesh, and in his sleep he was deeply aroused. And his maleness *was* throbbing.

A dual thunderclap, loud as the final trump, robbed him of his erection as he bolted upright in his bed. What the hell had that been?

Gunshots crackled into the pale dawn immediately after. After-echoes of the explosions racketed off the hills. Christ! It had to be Rebecca Caldwell. But how? Roger dressed hurriedly, careless for once of his appearance, sure only that the gunbelt fit his waist and the .45 Colt in its holster rested easily and was ready to come into play. He yanked on boots and ran from his room into the central courtyard of the hacienda.

Others had preceeded him. El Coronel, face black with rage and small eyes darting around for someone to blame, stalked toward the confused Styles. His words cut sharply.

"It would appear you were right, Don Rogelio. Your nemesis has returned. And with a vengeance, I'd say."

"Where did those explosions come from?" Roger inquired.

"The corral. Our horses have stampeded and are running around inside the wall. If the main gate had been open, they would have escaped. I sent men to try to calm the animals."

"Good. Thank you for acting so quickly." Roger had started to regain his composure. "From the sound of it, our men are engaging the enemy."

"They are. You could never guess who that enemy is."

"Rebecca Caldwell, of course."

"Perhaps. Try also some fifty or so Diegueño peons who have been turned into warriors."

202

"How can that be? How could they have gotten here when I sent Rudolfo to attack their village?"

"No doubt over his dead body. We'd better start getting control, or we'll be wiped out in half an hour," Ordaz snapped.

Pandemonium whirled through the compound. Horses, showing the whites of their eyes, ran shrieking around the space between the outer wall and the buildings. Most of the outlaw band had been compelled to flatten themselves against the scant shelter provided and make useless gestures in attempts to slow the stampede. Here and there, a few managed to position themselves so that they could fire at their so far unseen enemy.

Rifles crackled to life at the slightest sign of movement. An answering cloud of arrows descended on the exposed bandits. Several howled in pain as the crude points bit into their flesh. Cursing, their companions shot again at nothing visible. One of Ordaz's men, a former *vaquero*, decided he had a way to end the hazard from the horses.

With the help of a friend, he scaled to the top of a porch overhang on the cookshed. There he crouched until he sized up the whirling circle of terrified animals. That one, he decided. Already many of the creatures had begun to take orderly formation around one particular horse. When it swung in close by him, Estaban Lopez, the bow-legged ex-*vaquero*, began to time its actions.

On the next pass it came even closer. One more would do it.

Caught by surprise, the frightened horse had deviated and taken a short way instead of the full circle, Esteban nearly lost his chance. The big black thundered by only a foot out from the porch roof. Esteban flexed his legs and sprang outward.

He landed astride the demented beast, which began to hunch its back and crowhop to the side. Without saddle or reins, Esteban Lopez fought to maintain his precarious perch. Esteban heard the menacing whir of the arrow a moment before it struck the animal's front shoulder. Rearing upward on hind legs, the horse easily dumped its rider.

Eyes wide with horror, mouth open for a scream, Esteban Lopez fell under the hoofs of the running beasts behind. Unmindful of the grisly results, the fear-maddened animals pounded Esteban into a thick paste of mud, blood, and bone.

"Ian, if a message can be sent on an arrow, could an explosive charge?"

Ian reflected on this possibility a moment. "Not a charge of any size. Most likely not even a whole stick of dynamite. Too nose-heavy. But . . . half a stick might do it."

"Could you put some tacks and pieces of broken horseshoe in it?"

"Easily. At least, I think so."

"Will you give it a try now? I'd like to take out that front gate and then start using them on the bandits."

A wild, highland grin spread on Ian's face. "We'll see, my love."

While Ian labored on his new invention, Rebecca turned her attention to the matter of attacking the entrenched outlaws. She summoned Juan and two other leaders among the Diegueños.

"We're going to have to rush that place, horses or no," she began. "If enough warriors remain here to draw their attention, the gate will be the easiest place to gain entrance. With any luck, Ian may come up with a means for blowing it apart like the other."

"That's good, Rebecca," Juan allowed. "Our men are ready. It would be nice, though, if most of them will be able to go home to their wives."

"I think they will. Pick your best marksmen and have them make ready to put down a heavy volume of fire. Make the bandits think we're still in one place. The rest will gather over there, inside that line of trees opposite the main gate. Whoever is in charge of the ones remaining will start counting to ten and repeat it ten times when the rest leave. When he's counted that far, we'll rush the gate when they open fire."

"There's much danger in that."

"I know it, Juan. Right now, though, I can't come up with any other idea."

"Ready to try this, Becky," Ian declared happily.

The first bow launch fell short. Ian adjusted the positioning of the heavy stick closer to the center of the shaft and another try was made.

This time the arrow arched over the wall and landed near the cookshack. A shower of decomposed granite and horse droppings flew into the air when the dynamite went off.

"That's it! We did it," Ian chortled gleefully.

"Now, move down where you have a better shot at the gate," Rebecca instructed. "Then blow it off its hinges."

It took three shots. The last of them shattered nearly a third of the horizontal rails of the gate and it fell into the dirt. When the dust cleared, the frightened, milling horses located the opening and began to stream in that direction. Tails high and hooves flying, they left the scene of noise and pain.

"Stop them!" Roger Styles shouted. "For God's sake hold them back or we'll all be afoot."

More arrow-borne bombs began to fall inside the

compound. Their explosions created a bedlam of tortured sound. Dust and smoke filled the air as the men tried vainly to stop the escape of the horses. Sensing the hopelessness of it all, Pablo Ordaz began to yell at the men in an attempt to rally them.

"There'll be an attack any time now. Make ready. Forget the horses. *Olvidarse de los caballos!*" he repeated in Spanish. "You men, get to the wall. Hurry."

Roger reluctantly accepted the inevitable and began roughly to shove disoriented gunmen toward defensive positions along the adobe barrier. "Get up there. Stand on some adobe blocks. Keep a sharp eye," he demanded.

"We're ready to attack through the gate, Rebecca," Juan Lachusa informed the White Squaw.

"Good. I'll join your men in a moment." She turned to Ian. "Have your archers continue to launch dynamite into the compound until you see us get inside. Then stop. Same for the marksmen keeping the bandits occupied. Once we have a foothold, charge with them as well."

Hoofbeats pounded across a meadow to the south. Rebecca looked in that direction and made out the broad-shouldered frame of Lone Wolf. Excitement flared in her breast. Certain of success with the addition of fresh troops, she hurried to meet the tall, blond Crow warrior.

"Just in time," Rebecca called out to him.

"Glad to be of service," Lone Wolf answered through a grin. "What do you have in mind?"

"We're going to attack through that open gate." Rebecca pointed.

Lone Wolf's eyes widened. "What happened to it? Don't tell me. Ian and his . . ."

"Nasty bombs," Rebecca concluded.

"How soon? We've ridden hard and are tired. It's near to noon. Everyone could use a good meal."

Rebecca assumed a stricken expression. "I'd not given any thought to that. I wanted to hit them before any could get away."

Lone Wolf studied the besieged compound. "They're not going anywhere. Not for a while at least. We can afford an hour."

"*Por Dios*, there's more of them rode up," Pablo Ordaz swore. "Diegueños and Cahuillas. There's an army of Indians out there."

"Not to mention someone with a whole lot of dynamite," Roger replied dryly. "I'm sorry to have to admit it, but we're under siege."

"That's not so bad as it might seem," Ordaz declared. "They can last there only so long. My brother, Jaime, is nearby to here, waiting in the hills. He's bound to hear the sounds of battle. When he rides here, he can attack them in the rear, create confusion and fear. Then we shall smash them."

Chapter 23

Five of the bow-propelled bombs landed inside the compound a few minutes after one o'clock in the afternoon. Three more came quickly behind, followed by five more. The blasts rolled into one continuous rampage of horrendous noise. Dizzy and disoriented, blinded by dust and smoke, assailed by bits of metal and flying grains of decomposed granite, the outlaws staggered away from the outer wall, hands over their ears or with fingers gingerly digging at fragments of foreign matter buried in the skin of their faces. Another three explosions rocked the ground.

Gripped by fear, their internal balance disrupted by quaking ground shocks, several bandits turned away to void their stomachs. All along the line, men bled from their ears and tears ran involuntarily. Vomiting became epidemic. Another horrifying crash of five blasts pounded between the walls and the cookshack roof collapsed.

A shower of dust and steam erupted and agonized howls came from the scalded cook. He staggered into the open in time to have his pain taken away by a .45-70 slug from a Springfield civilian model rifle in the hands of a keen-eyed Diegueño youth of seventeen. Immediately rifles and muskets opened a continuous rattle from the concealing trees beyond the wall. Another barrage of flying bombs crashed onto target.

"It's time to go," Rebecca said calmly.

Mounted on their own horses, the attackers streamed across open ground toward Casa Rogelio. Despite the heavy volleys of rifle fire and relentless descent of dynamite bombs, the superior numbers of the defenders and their strong position soon began to tell. Three Diegueños fell first, blown out of the saddle by men sent to defend the front gate.

Six Cahuillas cut diagonally across the line of attack and rushed at the outlaws who fired from the wall. Two of them died at once, then three went down to an unusually disciplined volley. The survivor turned tail and streaked back to the main line of advance.

"It's almost like attacking soldiers," Rebecca yelled over the tumult.

"Too much so, for my liking," Lone Wolf concurred. "We'll have to turn back."

"That or lose too many men. It's those thick walls. The bandits can't be hit, except in the head. Too small a target from horseback."

"Pull back!" Rebecca called to the others. She fired her six-gun into the air, the agreed-upon retreat signal, and then again. The charge faltered, swung to the right and galloped away from the walls. Tears of frustration stung Rebecca's eyes, though she never shed them. Only another fifty yards and they would have been inside.

"It sounds like an army fighting up ahead," Manuel Gerrón remarked to Jaime Ordaz.

"Yes. Only those who remain at the hacienda don't have any artillery. We'd better sweep around to the south and come at the rancho from the west. I'd not like any nasty surprises to catch up to us, eh?"

"Nor I, Jaime. We've enough men here to tip the

scale if there's trouble. It would be a shame to waste that advantage."

"You're a wise man, Manuel. I must speak to my brother about putting you in charge of some raids."

"I'm flattered, Jaime. Ah, and, thank you for your praise."

Jaime shrugged. "It is nothing. Competence should be rewarded. We'll turn south in that next canyon, cross the ridge and come at the hacienda from an angle that will give us a chance for surprise."

It had taken a while to drag the heavy-laden wagons this far. Sheriff Hunsaker sweated along with his men, mostly volunteers who had formed a large posse at Alonzo Horton's insistence.

"I have to agree with Alonzo," Hunsaker told his chief deputy, Al Carl. "A hundred or so brigands loose in the back country is more than we can tolerate. Even so, this does seem more like a military campaign than a posse."

Chief Deputy Carl smiled broadly. He accepted the sheriff's evaluation of their situation. He also considered himself fortunate to have been chosen to come along. For once, the under-sheriff had been left in charge of the office and the many situations that could arise in the rest of the county. Here, though, Al Carl had an opportunity to make quite a name for himself. What they were up to would be news throughout California. It wouldn't hurt the prospects of an ambitious lawman to be a part of it.

"There's not a hundred of them who could stand against us," Carl said confidently. "Forty-five men and a dozen sailors, along with those two six-pound cannons from that merchant ship of Alonzo Horton's. Odds are they'll throw up their hands and we can take 'em without a fight."

"Don't be too sure, Al," Hunsaker cautioned. "From what I've heard, this big-time bandit from Baja, El Coronel, has joined up with Roger Styles. They've fought the Mexican Army several times and came out on top. I don't think they'd hesitate to take us on."

"We'll be ready for 'em," Carl returned through a grin.

From ahead came thumps and rumbles. To some in the posse, who had fought in the War between the States, it sounded like distant artillery. Sheriff Hunsaker had an idea what it might be, though he kept his own council.

"We'll be there in another two hours and find out for ourselves," he remarked to his chief deputy.

"I can hardly wait," Al Carl responded enthusiastically.

"We have to attack again," Rebecca Caldwell insisted. "Any longer and they'll be over the shock of our initial assault."

"You talk disconcertingly like a colonel I once knew," Lone Wolf responded. "We have to keep our own losses down. Roger and his hardcases are caught inside the hacienda. Their supplies will run low before very long. We can hold the line out here and starve them out."

"A siege? Is it even possible in modern times?" Ian queried.

"You can believe it," Lone Wolf answered.

"What's to say that all of Roger's bandits are in there?" Rebecca suggested. "A siege depends on having *all* of the enemy pinned down. We could be surprised by some of the men sent out after us earlier on."

"It still offers the best choice," Lone Wolf insisted.

"We may live to regret it," Ian offered in support of Rebecca.

"More likely, if we're caught, we won't live to regret

it," the White Squaw quipped. Her shoulders sagged slightly as she relented. "All right. Spread the men out to cover every possible way out of the hacienda. Have them conserve ammunition. We'll have to send for food and supplies if this lasts long."

"Easier for us than for Roger," Lone Wolf reminded.

"That's the one advantage we have," Rebecca admitted.

This would be easy, Jaime Ordaz gloated as he looked through the screen of trees at the backs of crouched Indians, weapons ready, who gazed at the distant wall of the hacienda. They'd never expect such a move. He nodded in satisfaction and licked his lips.

"Make ready to attack them," he instructed Manuel Guerrón. "Have the men cover as wide an area as they can. Our first blow must be decisive."

"*Sí*, Jaime. It'll be done as you wish. Who gets to kill the *gringa*?"

"Whomever God wills, *amigo*. In fighting of this sort, there's no time to make choices. If she survives, I think it will be a long time before death visits her." Jaime grinned evilly. "And her *panocha* will be sore as hell."

"What the hell!" Al Carl exploded in a whisper. "*Bandidos* attacking the Styles's place?"

"I don't think so," Sheriff Hunsaker advised his chief deputy. "Look beyond them. Isn't that the Caldwell woman in the buckskin dress? Looks like they're about to be hit in the rear." Hunsaker made a quick decision.

"Tell the gun crews to stay by their cannon. The rest get ready to take on those Mexican bandits. When I take a shot at one of them, that'll be the signal to wade in."

Rebecca Caldwell paced back and forth. An itch had

formed between her shoulderblades and she felt as though a hundred eyes watched her back. She came to where Ian worked on two large explosive packages and squatted beside him.

"Ian, I have the strangest feeling that we're not out here alone."

"Don't feel a thing, myself. Who could it be? Say, it might be the sheriff from San Diego."

"Ummmm," Rebecca considered. "That could be, yes. Only . . ." Her voice trailed off in the loud report of a rifle.

"Sheriff's posse!" a voice bellowed. "Throw down your guns and put up your hands."

Immediately a battle erupted between the line of attacking Diegueños and the distant voice. Rebecca saw fleeting shapes among the trees and brush. Men in Mexican costume. Bullets slashed through the leaves and clipped small branches from manzanita and oak.

"Down!" Rebecca shouted. "Everyone get down. If you have a clear shot at the bandits, use it. Be careful, the sheriff and his men are over there to the west."

Trapped in the crossfire, the bandit force dwindled rapidly. Men shouted and cursed, screamed, and died. Powder smoke lay in a thick blanket that undulated in the hot, lazy air. A pocket of resistance formed around Jaime Ordaz. Those who failed to reach it met death individually. Soon Anglos, in an assortment of city clothes, could be distinguished in the brush. With a wild howl, Jaime Ordaz broke free on his broadchested mount and raced toward the open gateway to the hacienda.

Half a dozen men streamed after him. Among them, Manuel Gerrón, Paco Nuñez and Umberto Duran. A few more fought their way clear to reinforce the beleaguered defenders by a total of eleven.

"Well, they're all in there now," Lone Wolf said dryly.

213

"And the sheriff is here," Rebecca reminded him.

"Miss Caldwell, Reverend Claymore, Mr. Baylor," the tall, lean lawman acknowledged them a short while later. "I see you have the rascals penned up."

"That we do," Rebecca answered brightly.

"Fine, then. In a short while we should be able to blast them out quite easily."

"How do you mean?"

"I've brought along two six-pound cannon and their crews."

Twenty minutes later, the two ships' cannon began to pound the walls. Eyes red with fury, Pablo Ordaz sought out Roger Styles.

"I thought you said they had no artillery. What is that, *imbécil?*"

A roundshot howled through the air and blasted away the cupola of the bell tower at one corner of the hacienda. The big bronze bell gave off mournful tones as it tumbled down the shattered ruin of adobe blocks.

Desperately, Roger Styles wished to be somewhere else.

Chapter 24

With a twanging bark sharp as that of an enraged mastiff and loud as doomsday's knell, the pair of six pounders discharged again and again. Mounds of dirt flew into the air. Under cover of this terrible barrage and a scything slash of gunfire, four Diegueño volunteers ran forward with the heavy packages containing the last of Ian's dynamite.

Following directions, they set them solidly against the wall ends at each side of the wide main gate. They hurriedly piled stones and dirt atop them, then yanked at the exposed tabs of friction igniters. The fuses sputtered to life while they dashed wildly back to the protection of their own lines.

When the explosions came, followed immediately by twin bursting shells, mighty chunks of the wall disappeared in a fountain of powdered adobe. Mounted now, Rebecca's force, augmented by two-thirds of the posse, galloped toward the breach. Those left behind gave out a ragged cheer and went back to sniping at the defenders. The sailors manned their cannon again and concentrated on the large main building.

Case shot began to powder the hacienda wall, though it would take more time and ammunition to penetrate three feet of adobe. The gunners adjusted their aim, and the next two rounds blasted through thick wooden shutters and exploded inside the house. Screams of pain and horror rose over the tumult. On a command from Ian Claymore, the crews ceased fire as Rebecca and her howling band raced into the space between the outer defenses and the hacienda.

Fighting swirled everywhere. Lone Wolf and half of the Diegueños swung wide to the right and hurtled toward the barn, where many of the outlaws had taken shelter. Bullets gouged the ground, sending up spurts of decomposed granite dust. One cracked close by Lone Wolf's head and he ducked low, swinging his tomahawk left-handed as he did.

The keen edge of the 'hawk slashed the features off the face of a *bandido*. Wailing, the man put a hand to the grisly remains, feeling the exposed bone of his skull. Shock mercifully rendered him unconscious before he bled to death. The attack rolled on. From the opposite direction, Lone Wolf heard cries of alarm and the moans of wounded men. Rebecca must be doing all right.

To Rebecca's right, the blasted cookshack lay only a dozen yards away. Dimly through the smoke and dust Rebecca made out a form flitting from the window casement to the doorway. She timed the motion automatically and sent off a .44 slug to intersect with the next appearance in the doorway.

A bandit cried out and rebounded backward from the impact of hot lead. Grimly satisfied, Rebecca turned in her saddle and sought another target. Plenty presented themselves.

Four men rushed at the invaders, weapons blazing. Rebecca raised her Smith American to return fire. A powerful blow struck her right shoulder, and a moment later white-hot pain radiated out from the spot. The bullet's impact flung the Smith .44 away from her open hand. The realization that she had been hit, and badly,

216

momentarily stunned her into immobility.

"We got her! We got her," the outlaw scum cried jubilantly.

One of them learned otherwise when Rebecca recovered voluntary motion and drew the second Smith American left-handed. She eared back the hammer and let it fall on a fresh cartridge. The bullet split Bert Conlin's sternum and sent showers of bone slivers into his lungs. He bent impossibly backward when the avenging lead severed his spinal cord.

Legs drumming uncontrollably, Bert flopped on the ground until life left him. Queasy from her wound, Rebecca turned aside.

"We have to get out of here," Roger yelled in panic.

Acrid fumes of black powder smoke filled the thick-walled dining room of the hacienda. Women wailed and mopped at surface wounds that streamed blood. Several corpses littered the interior where the deadly rounds from the cannon had exploded. Somewhere in this madhouse Pablo Ordaz still directed resistance to the powerful force that had attacked them. Roger sought him in desperation.

"They're too many," Roger declared when he located the Mexican bandit. "We have to pull out or we'll all die."

"I'm in full agreement, *amigo*," El Coronel said sarcastically. "Only how do you propose we get away without being dismembered by those cannon?"

"If we don't get away now, we never will," Roger insisted.

Ordaz considered it a moment. "My brother Jaime is holding the barn. If we rally the people left in here and make a dash for it, we might succeed."

"We *have to*," Roger urged, voice sharp-edged with rising fright.

217

"All right, then." Quickly Pablo Ordaz set about gathering all who could still walk and fight.

They'd have one chance, and only one, he knew.

With blurring vision, Rebecca saw furtive movement along one side of the hacienda. Human forms resolved themselves in her pain-dampened mind. Among them she thought she recognized Roger Styles. How heavy the Smith American felt as she raised the .44 revolver in her left hand. Perspiration broke out on her forehead.

"Damn!" The curse escaped her. She seemed unable to hold still, swaying in the saddle.

It all took so much time. Fuzzy, the slightly pear-shaped figure of Roger Styles appeared in her sight picture. Brow creased in concentration, she squeezed the trigger. The discharge nearly jerked the six-gun from her hand.

Roger Styles cried out pitifully when the bullet slammed into his left thigh and gouged away at the muscle. He sank to his knees and pressed his back against the wall.

"Oh, no. Don't let it happen to me. Please don't let me die here," he wailed, his earlier bravado entirely forgotten in the pain.

Rebecca aimed again as best she could and fired two more shots before the world appeared to whirl around her and she fell unconscious, from the saddle.

Bright fall sunlight streamed in through the open window. With it came the tangy-sweet scent of salt air. Crisply starched sheets crackled on the bed in a room of the Horton House as Rebecca Caldwell rolled onto her back from her left side and moaned slightly.

"She's coming around." A familiar voice filtered through the dampening cocoon that seemed to swath her head.

With effort, Rebecca forced her eyes to open. The brightness caused her to squint and try to bring up her right hand to shield her gaze. Pain lashed at her and nearly took away her consciousness.

"Take it easy, Becky," Ian Claymore urged her. "Doctor, she's come out of it for sure," he said to an unseen third party.

Price Knowlton, Alonzo Horton's personal physician, stepped into the range of Rebecca's hazy view. She made out Ian Claymore as well. Where . . . ? What . . . ? Questions she couldn't even ask assailed her.

"You're all right, Becky. You're at the Horton House. A corner room on the third floor, with a beautiful view of the bay."

"When d-did . . . ? Roger! Is he . . . ?"

"We brought you here after the battle ended. Roger Styles, Pablo Ordaz, and about ten others got away."

"But . . . I . . . I shot Roger. Three times, from . . . from as close as that wall." Rebecca's nod indicated the farthest wall, where a circular bow window looked out over San Diego Bay.

"You may have, but he managed to live through it. At least until he and the others slipped away through the chaparral into Baja California. If he's that severely wounded, chances are you've seen the last of him."

"Not . . . not until I stand beside his coffin," Rebecca forced out with her usual stubborn expression.

"You'd best rest a while now, young lady," Dr. Knowlton rumbled, fingers of his left hand fishing in his vest pocket for a watch, while his right ones grasped her wrist. "Mustn't excite yourself the first day."

"First day? How long ha-have I been here?"

"Two days since the fight," Ian informed her. "You lost a lot of blood and had a bit of a fever. You'd slip in and out of a coma, never quite aware of your surroundings. Yet, you'll be well now, I know it."

"If you'd listen to your doctor, instead of your sweetheart, young lady, you'd be told that the fight is far from over."

"Yes . . . I know . . . Roger's still out there. . . ."

Ian covered his face with his hands and groaned.

"Now you get on out of here," Dr. Knowlton fussed. "Reverend or not, she needs her rest." Then to Rebecca, "I was talkin' about your health, missy."

Five men, three of them Mexicans, rode quietly into San Diego late the same afternoon. They eschewed a livery stable and tied their horses on a side street, outside a saloon, some three blocks from the Horton House. They entered the barroom first to ritually wash away the trail dust before tending to their business in town.

"You're sure it's the Horton House *hotel*?" the tallest of the five, a lanky blond Anglo, demanded. "Not Horton's own house?"

"Positive, Señor Walsh. My cousin, she works at the hotel as a maid."

"Julio, we're only gonna have one chance at this. Anything goes wrong and I'll be lookin' up you and your cousin."

"It is—how you say?—a sure thing," Julio said, dismissing any worry. His hot, black eyes stared long at the *gringo*.

Dooley Walsh drained his glass and signaled for another beer. "This time gimme a rye chaser," he demanded.

Shortly before sundown, the five men relocated their horses, within a block of their intended destination, though separated from each other. They met near the rear entrance to the bustling establishment.

"Quietly," Julio urged. "My cousin will let us in, but we must not be seen by anyone. There is a back stair, for hotel workers to use. We can get to the room by that means."

Still a bit groggy, Rebecca Caldwell lay in her bed. The dull throb in her shoulder had reduced in intensity enough that she no longer grew faint from its persistent waves of pain. Lone Wolf had come to visit, likewise Ian, who had helped her feed herself a skimpy meal at suppertime. He'd only left minutes ago. It surprised her then when she heard footsteps in the hall that stopped outside her door. Furtive sounds followed that prickled an alarm at the back of her head. Wood splintered in the jamb when the flimsy portal flung violently open.

Three men bolted into the room. The one in the middle, a cold-eyed son of a bitch with dirty-blond hair hanging in lank curls and a nasty, crooked-toothed smile held his six-gun at the ready in his left hand.

"So you're that female terror, Rebecca Caldwell, eh? Looks like you caught a slug."

"Get out of my room," Rebecca demanded icily.

"Say now, listen to that," Dooley Walsh drawled to his companions. "The lady's real tough. Some friends of mine sent us here to see you died of complications from your wounds."

"Not this time, you bastard," Rebecca grated out.

Dooley Walsh didn't even have time to change his face into a startled expression before the diminutive .38 Smith Baby Russian spoke from under Rebecca's covers and a hot lead slug ripped up Dooley's right nostril and erupted with fiery havoc into his brain. Rebecca's second bullet poked a hole through his larynx and brought about a look of childlike hurt on the dying man's face. He stumbled to the side, tripped over a

221

footstool, and sprawled full length on the ornate Damascus carpet.

That left Julio Valdez with a clear shot. He raised the Colt .45 in a grimy fist and started to line up the sights. Loud explosions from behind him interrupted his concentration and he half turned to see the cause.

Gunsmoke made a thick, gray veil that obscured the view. The two men left outside to prevent surprise had fallen into each other and lay across the hall floor, shoulder to shoulder, wide scarlet pools forming from the ragged exit wounds in their sides.

"Hey, *bandido*, back in here," Rebecca called from the bed.

Julio turned back in time to see yellow-orange flame blossom from a smoking black hole in the bedspread. The bullet smacked into flesh an inch below his navel. Julio staggered back, tried to raise his revolver, and released a keening cry of agony. The fires of hell already ate at his bowels. Rebecca shot him again.

Still aimed low, the slug propelled Julio backward, so that his knees caught the windowsill and he crashed through the shattering glass to fall, screaming, to the street below. The scream seemed to last a long time.

Its sound served to unlock the third hardcase in the room. He whipped up his Merwin and Hulbert revolver and eared back the hammer. For all his hurry it did him no good. Rebecca's .38 round punched him solidly in the stomach and dropped the gunman to his knees. An instant later, a .44 Remington crashed loudly from the doorway and the big bullet turned the outlaw's head into a crimson splash. Ian Claymore rushed to Rebecca's side.

"Oh, darling, darling. Did . . . did they hurt you?"

"No. I'm fine, Ian." Then she burst into tears.

Ian patted her glossy black hair and spoke soothingly. After a minute, Rebecca regained her usual calm detachment and wiped away the last of her moment of weakness. Through wet lashes she saw Lone Wolf in the doorway.

"I . . . how did the two of you know?"

"Lone Wolf was on his way up to see you," Ian explained. "I came along to talk with him a while. We saw them break into your room from the stairwell. Lone Wolf got the first two. Then I ran down the hall. You . . . they . . . he nearly . . ."

"Yes. I didn't have time to reload and that was my last round."

"Let's hope that finishes off all of Roger's little animals," Lone Wolf said from the hallway.

He stepped into the room. "You look a mess, Rebecca. And that bedspread is going to start a regular fire if we don't do something."

"Oh, we shall, we shall," Rebecca replied, laughing.

Three days later, cheered by attentive visits by Alonzo Horton, Ian Claymore, and Lone Wolf, Rebecca was pronounced well enough to get up and around. Though she was not to consider travel for a while yet, Dr. Knowlton insisted. She sat in a lace-frilled frock at the small table in the restored bow window, watching ships sail gracefully over the placid waters of the bay. Children's shrill voices and the sounds of commerce rose from the streets below. She had been laboriously writing a list of things they had discovered about Roger Styles's plans that had not as yet been resolved. Too many possibilities to look into right yet, she thought regretfully. A knock took her from her task.

"Come in."

Ian Claymore entered, a hangdog expression on his face. He twisted his hat nervously and advanced hesitantly across the replacement rug that showed no signs of violent death.

"You've decided then what you are to do?" Rebecca stated flatly.

"Yes, I have. My calling is to administer to my flock. First and foremost I am a minister, Becky. I can't let down the board of deacons and the Presbytry. So, Hester and I shall be returning to Yuma and to my mission to the wild Scots and their Indian families."

"How . . . soon?"

"We, ah, leave in three days."

"I'll miss you, Ian."

"Not so much as I'll miss you. You were, er, are something . . . special, Becky. I'll never know another like you."

"We've been happy together, Ian. We could still be. . . ."

"Not if I failed myself in my own eyes. I can't . . . I shouldn't even be here now. I . . ."

Wretchedly he dropped his hat and reached out for her. Rebecca flung herself into his embrace, unmindful of the stab of pain it brought from her right shoulder. They kissed with flammable ardor, bodies pressed tightly together in a familiar and exciting posture. Rebecca twisted her lips away and began to fumble with the buttons of his vest.

Before long they stood naked, radiant in their passion, avidly examining the well-known and loved curves and contours of each other's glowing flesh. Ian took Rebecca's hand and led her to the bed.

Fully aroused, Ian trembled and buried his hands in her glossy black hair. Then he crossed the room and locked the door. Rebecca lay back and welcomed him with raised arms and widespread legs.

Who said partings had to be sad?

13—31—62—76—90—127—